I'd Tear Down the Stars

And other stories

David Hutto

Published by Pretense Press
Atlanta, Georgia, USA

ISBN: 978-0-9905692-2-0 (paperback)
ISBN: 978-0-9905692-3-7 (ebook)

"The Smallest Dreams in the City" was first published in *The Cimmerian Journal*.
"Snow Fool" was first published in *Skylark*.

Cover design: Aaron Davis, Booklogix.
Copy editing: Diana Plattner, Plaid Hat Books.
Proofreading: Maggie Parry, WordColor.

David Hutto is a
native of Georgia,
and after multiple
absences he currently
resides in Atlanta. On
his long and motley
resume, he can
include work as a
fried chicken cook, a
factory laborer on
four occasions, a
hospital laboratory
tech, a nursing home
attendant, a Russian
interpreter (including
volunteer work with
the Olympics in
1996), a cashier in a
home improvement
store, an editorial
assistant for a
publisher in New
York, an asbestos
abatement inspector,
a college professor of
English, and currently
as a medical copy
editor. Into these
stories he brings his
wide experience of

living—like it or
not—in a world
where sometimes you
thrive, and sometimes
you just survive.

His most recent publication is the novel *The Illusion of Being Here*.

Website: www.davidhutto.com
Blog: www.writeortakeanap.com

THE STORIES

The stories in this collection were written over a thirty-year period. They are set in a few of the places where I've lived (Georgia, North Carolina, New Jersey, and Pennsylvania), as well as places I didn't (Mexico, the moon). I've included variety here in styles of writing as well as topics, and a person might ask, "So what are these stories about?" That has an easy answer. They're about people making their way through life trying to figure out how to be here.

Like most of us.

I dedicate these stories to people who have read my writing and encouraged me, sometimes with a heart full of support, sometimes in small ways, and I'm grateful for all of it.

And these stories are also dedicated to people who have known what it is like to struggle and work hard just to go forth each day, not always sure what the point is. I have sailed in that boat.

CONTENTS

I'd Tear Down the Stars

The oldest memory she had was of people riding seahorses and eating almonds. It couldn't be a real memory, of course, but when she went drifting down through recollections, of childhood back in North Dakota, of the blue swing set in her grandparents' yard, of her father getting stung by a bumblebee, which she was told happened when she was two years old, the people on seahorses seemed to come before all of them. What this mysterious memory was she didn't know, but she dreamed about it sometimes. She was dreaming now of the seahorse riders, moving through blue waves, as she slept on the bus crossing the Coahuila desert.

The bus hit a hole in the road, bounced, and shook her. As the dream faded away, recent memories swirled into its place: buying the last Beatles' album, feeding a homeless dog, watching the war in Vietnam on TV. Liv came fully awake now

9

and looked through the window at the darkness outside. Yes, she was in Mexico, her first time in another country. Off the roadway a white house stood, with a single light above the door casting a pool of light on the white wall of the house and on the reddish earth of the ground in front. A bicycle leaned up against the wall of the house. Otherwise, the night was moonless and dark, and the desert was mostly invisible. The sky was brilliant with stars, like powdered sugar blown ferociously onto dark cloth, leaving the sky with swirls and splotches where the stars were more dense. Liv had never seen such a thing, and it was almost frightening to imagine the enormity of it.

She yawned and sat up a bit, then reached to the seat beside her, where her large cloth bag lay. She felt thirsty and fumbled inside the bag for the small aluminum canteen. All of her possessions were in the bag: a long cotton skirt that she'd tie-dyed, like the one she was wearing; two more blouses; three pairs of panties; a passport; a small metal flashlight, given to her by her grandmother; a large wooden comb; a red leather snap purse with $321 and some pesos she had forgotten to count; a black-and-white photograph of John Lennon; a paperback copy of Carlos Castaneda's *The Teachings of Don Juan;* and a plastic zip-up bag with roll-on deodorant, a toothbrush, toothpaste, and two packages of antacid tablets, as she knew she had a delicate stomach. She pulled out the canteen, took a small drink, and screwed the metal cap back on.

"That's Orion," she heard the man across the aisle saying. He was talking to his daughter, pointing out stars. The man's wife and other daughter were asleep in the seat behind. "You see that bright star?" he said to his daughter. "That's Betelgeuse, and from there his arm goes up to the left. You see? No? Lean over here and follow my finger."

Liv shifted in her seat and the man heard her. He looked over and said, "Do you like astronomy? I was just showing Jill how to find some of the constellations."

11

"I never learned any of that," Liv said. She didn't talk much to strangers. For that matter, she didn't talk much even with people she knew.

"Astronomy is a fascinating subject," he said. "The stars are another one of God's wonders." Liv didn't reply, and the man turned back to the window. "That's Taurus," he said, pointing out the window. "Taurus means 'bull.'" The bus was about half full, and no one else was talking that Liv could hear. They occasionally hit a rough spot in the road, and by the faint light coming from the dashboard she could see the shapes of the passengers rock in their seats. Most people were either sleeping or sitting silently.

The man looking at stars was named Frank Holland, the daughter beside him was Jill, the younger girl was Amy, and his wife was Linda. This family was from Macon, Georgia, and had gotten on the bus back in the town of Saltillo when it was still light. Liv remembered that Linda and both daughters were wearing patterned dresses, while Frank had on a white short-sleeved shirt but with a tie. Liv had been sitting with her feet out, partially blocking the aisle, and as they came down the narrow row between the seats, she moved and instinctively said, "Excuse me." She didn't know how to say that in Spanish anyway, didn't know more than three or four words of the language. As she moved out of the way, she was surprised when the man said, "Oh, you're American. I might have guessed that from your blond hair."

After the family had gotten seated, he had turned and begun talking to Liv as though she would be glad to meet other Americans in this unlikely place, in this second-class bus headed to the small town of Parras de la Fuente. She was not glad to meet other Americans, however. She didn't mind that they were American, she just didn't want to have a long conversation with people she didn't know. Still, she had listened as Frank talked. He had told her they were from Georgia, that he was a hotel manager back in Macon. He seemed to like to talk about his daughters, who appeared to Liv to be about ten and eight years old. Frank told Liv that Jill had won a best-student award last year and that the youngest, Amy, spoke better Spanish than anybody in the family. "I'm going to have to catch up with her," he said. "I've got to do some fast learning, if I'm going to do what I came here for. We're with Good Word Missions, and we're going to Parras to help spread the word of God."

"You're missionaries?" Liv had asked.

"That's right. Good Word Missions." He leaned slightly across the aisle and lowered his voice, as if he were telling her a secret. Other people on the bus all seemed to be locals, or at least people speaking Spanish, and their clothes were different from what Liv was accustomed to, with different fabrics and brighter colors.

"The people in Parras follow fortune tellers and what you might call witch doctors," Frank had said to Liv. He had looked out the window, then said, "We want to bring them the true word of God. So where are you from?"

"North Dakota."

"Well, you're a long way from home."

She hadn't told him that she had not lived there for a year, that she had been with her friend John on a commune in Colorado with seventeen other people. She said nothing about her life there either, trying to learn to spin wool from the sheep they raised, or that she had realized she would never be a spinner. And she didn't tell him that she was on her way to look for a wise man, Isandro de Pereda, one of the "fortune tellers" who lived in Parras de la Fuente.

Sitting now in the dark bus, she took out her canteen for another sip of water. Frank was still giving an astronomy lesson to his daughter. "Very good, honey." The two of them were looking out the window at the stars. "That's right."

Liv closed her eyes and drifted back into herself. For days she had been on buses, an endless ride, and she was glad it was nearly over. She remembered the ride out of Colorado, across Texas, down to Laredo, remembered every person she had seen along the way. It was only a few days ago that she'd left

15

Colorado, with instructions on how to find Isandro de Pereda when she got to Parras, and now most of the ride was a memory. Already life on the commune seemed strangely distant, as if it had never happened, somehow more distant than the year she had spent after high school in her home town of Velva, working as a receptionist for an eye doctor.

Liv had sometimes wondered if suicide was a good thing, something like going on to another dimension. She had thought of ways people might kill themselves, but if she had stayed at that job in Velva she wouldn't have needed to kill herself, she would have fallen down dead of boredom. Two of her closest friends had left Velva. Gary was drafted to go to Vietnam, where he died in Nixon's war of imperialism. Before Gary had gone to Vietnam, her friend John left to move to the People of Light commune in Colorado, and after Gary was killed, she followed John, to the dismay of her mother and the stunned amazement of her father. The only reason she gave them for leaving Velva was "I'm not happy here", which they didn't understand. How could anyone not be happy in Velva? That's how they saw things. At the commune she wasn't bored anymore, but she couldn't say she was happier there. She wasn't especially happy anywhere, and she couldn't really imagine being happy.

At the commune she had also met Rollo, who said he was a combination of cowboy and hippie. "I ride horses and smoke dope," he said, and he showed her how to do both. He'd also lived in San Francisco for a while, went to see the Grateful Dead and Janis Joplin, and he told stories that sounded simply fantastical and magical to Liv. It was Rollo who'd told her about Isandro de Pereda, an old man he had met in Mexico.

"He lives outside of town in a big yellow house," Rollo said, "with his kids and grandkids. It's kind of like a Mexican commune. Sometimes they get together in the evening and somebody plays guitar and they sing songs. The family grows grapes, and they sell them to a winery in town. That's how they live."

The idea of living in a big yellow house, of grapes and wine, of a family that sang, this all sounded remarkable to Liv, almost unreal. It was sure nothing like Velva, North Dakota, growing up in a white wooden house and going to the Lutheran church every Sunday.

"People come to Isandro's house every day," Rollo said. "It's kind of like enlightenment classes on the patio. Isandro knows a lot about the earth and about the kind of energy that comes from the earth. So anybody that shows up he'll teach them about it. I was there for a month, and I learned a lot about how to be. Just, you know, how to be, how to feel the life force from the earth." How to be. That's what Liv wanted. If you knew how to be, would you be unhappy? It didn't strike her that not speaking Spanish would be a real problem. Wisdom is beyond what language you speak. The Beatles even went to India looking for wisdom, so you didn't have to stay in your own country to find it.

The bus rocked her back to sleep, and as she was drifting off, she remembered seeing Rollo, wearing his cowboy hat, standing down by the sheep pen last spring. He'd been with his girlfriend, Moon Sky. Liv sank deeper into sleep and the memory turned into a dream where Rollo looked very serious and Moon Sky was crying.

"What's wrong?" Liv said in the dream, although she couldn't hear her own voice.

"The Beatles are breaking up. They just announced it on the radio."

Then both Moon Sky and Rollo began crying.

A noise woke her up. Or was it lack of noise? As she came to consciousness, she found that the bus was sitting still and quiet, the motor off. Sometimes they had stopped to pick up passengers or to let someone off, but it was completely dark outside, the driver was gone, and the bus was mostly empty. The missionary family was gone. A few people were asleep and an old woman was looking toward the door. From out in the darkness came another a noise, a shout, closer this time. In a minute the driver ran onto the bus, jumped into his seat, and started the motor. As the bus lurched forward, he turned the wheel sharply to the right, pulled forward about a hundred yards, then stopped. He left the bus running, with the lights shining forward, and got off again. A number of people stood starkly lit by the headlights, and Liv recognized the missionary mother, Linda, with her daughters.

When the bus stopped, Linda turned around and ran up the steps, and with a quick, tense voice nearly shouted, "Does anyone have a light? We need a light."

Even though Liv was puzzled and a little afraid of what was happening, she was aware that Linda had asked in English on a bus with people who spoke Spanish. "Yes," Liv said, "I've got a flashlight."

"Please," Linda said, and started down the aisle toward Liv, but Liv had found the flashlight in her bag and was already moving toward the front.

"What's going on?" she asked.

"Frank might be hurt," Linda said, and taking the flashlight, she ran off the bus.

Liv followed her and joined the group of people standing in the bright headlights. One of the men took the flashlight and moved off into the darkness, with other people moving gingerly forward behind him. There was a sharp drop-off ahead, and the man stood at the edge, shone the light down, then called out. Several other men, accompanied by Linda, moved carefully to the dark edge of the ravine. Linda screamed, then turned back toward the bus. The youngest girl, Amy, was crying, and both girls moved close to their mother.

"Is Daddy OK?" Amy said, but Linda just put her arms around her without saying anything. Liv felt like she must be the only other person on the bus who spoke English, so she should probably make herself available to be talked to. She walked over and stood near Linda and the girls, but hoped they would not say anything to her.

Using Liv's small flashlight, several men went off to the right, where they could climb down into the ravine. It was a slow business, as they shone the light back and forth to try to see where they were going, and they even passed the light back and forth between them. Slowly they made their way to where Frank had fallen off the edge of the ravine. Getting him back up was even more difficult. The distance was not great, but the entire process took a long time. When they finally got him up and into the bus lights, Liv looked at him a moment in the harsh bright headlights, then looked away, feeling ill. His head was hanging loose, and his face was bloody. She leaned over to say to Linda, "I'll take the girls back on the bus."

"Yes," Linda said, but looked only toward her husband.

Liv led the stunned girls back onto the bus, toward the back. Amy was crying, but Jill, the older girl, though she looked stricken, had not yet cried. In a few minutes, people got back on the bus, and after some discussion, mysterious and in Spanish, three men pulled Frank's body up into the front seat, where it slumped against the window. The unpleasant idea struck Liv that when they started driving, his head would be bouncing against the window, but he wouldn't feel it. Linda stood beside her husband for a few minutes, kneeling down at one point, but as the bus pulled back onto the highway, she came back to where Liv sat with the girls. When Linda sat down, Amy went over and climbed into her mother's lap. The little girl closed her eyes and put her thumb in her mouth. Jill stayed in the seat beside Liv.

"What are we going to do?" Jill said softly, but Liv didn't answer.

A few minutes after the bus was on the road again, one of the passengers came back to Linda and said, "Town soon."

"Parras?" Linda asked.

"Sí," he said, "Parras." Then he returned to his seat.

After a few minutes of silence, Jill said, "He wanted to look at the stars."

"What?" Liv said.

"Daddy walked off in the dark to look at the stars. That's when he fell."

"Why was the bus stopped?" Liv asked.

"I don't know. Daddy said the driver was checking the bus, and we could get out for a few minutes. He was looking at the stars and he fell." Now she began to cry, but softly.

They rode without speaking another twenty minutes or so until they began passing buildings, coming into the town of Parras de la Fuente. Though it was still dark, Liv looked out the window, her interest mixed with odd emotions from the strange event she had become a part of. Looking out at the dark shapes of Parras, she remembered stories from Rollo about this town, the final destination of her own long trip. His stories of what the town would be like did not match the strange circumstances. The memories were wrong.

Instead of going to the bus station, the driver drove to the police station and went inside to talk to one of the officers, who came out to the bus. The officer saw Frank's body and came

24

back to try to talk to Linda, but he didn't know English, and Linda's Spanish was slight, even if she had not been so distressed. Finally the officer just held out his hands and made a gentle motion to Linda to stay where she was. He then rode on the bus to the morgue.

While Frank's body was being taken off the bus, his family stood to get off as well. To Liv's surprise, Jill turned to her and said, "Come with us." Liv looked at her, and Jill said, "Please? Come with us. What are we going to do?"

Liv hesitated a second, then said, "I'm coming." She picked up her bag of belongings and went down the aisle behind them, wondering what she could do herself.

At the morgue, efforts to communicate were futile, but Linda was offered the use of a telephone, which she accepted. She went into an office, where she talked to someone in English, but not loud enough to be understood outside. In a few minutes Linda came out to the waiting area where Liv and the girls sat. "I called Alphonso back in Saltillo," she said to her daughters.

Then she turned to Liv. "It's someone we know from the mission. He's going to drive over." She stopped and looked at the floor, then back up at Liv. "Thank you for staying with us."

Liv felt uncomfortable and didn't know how to reply. "Your daughter asked me to," she said.

"Thank you," Linda repeated. She looked out the window where the faint edge of morning was coming up from the east. Some brighter stars were still visible. "I'd rip out every one of those stars to undo this," she said. She didn't seem to be speaking to anyone in particular.

Liv sat with the family for two hours, until Alphonso arrived from Saltillo. He hugged Linda and both girls, then went in to speak to one of the morgue workers.

Wondering if her role here, whatever it was, had ended, Liv stood up and said, "I guess I'll be going. Your friend is here to help, and he speaks Spanish."

"Alright," Linda said. Jill came over and gave Liv a hug.

Liv bent down closer to Jill's level and said, "I'm sorry about your dad." Jill nodded and didn't say anything.

It was now early morning and traffic was in the streets. Liv walked along, unsure just where to go. She was tired and hungry, and her stomach felt strange from a night of being awake. When she passed a cafe, she stopped to have a roll with cheese and a glass of mango juice. Exhaustion was coming on, and from being tired, from being in such a foreign place, and from the mysterious tragedy she had just seen, she felt as if she were in a dream. The food was set down in front of her, she took a bite of the roll, chewing slowly, and closed her eyes.

After eating she left the cafe, but two doors down she stopped to look at the building beside her. On the pale yellow wall was a painting of two blue and green birds, and beside them a badly painted head of a woman wearing a large necklace. Above the door in gold letters outlined in black was the word *Fortunas*. Even without knowing Spanish, Liv guessed that this was a fortune teller, one of the people Frank had been coming

27

here to work against. She thought of him as he had first gotten on the bus, so full of life and energy, and now he lay in the morgue. Or was that only the body? Was he somewhere else?

A heaviness came over Liv, as if she couldn't walk any more, but she lifted her unwilling steps, sighing. After a few minutes of walk, she was surprised to find that the bus station was ahead of her. Turning and looking around at the town, Liv sighed, then went into the station. At the ticket window, she said, "Nuevo Laredo," gave the woman pesos to pay for her ticket and sat down in the waiting area. She thought about the strange events of the past few hours and waited for the bus to begin her return home.

See the Jungle When It's Wet with Rain

Sometimes a house on fire is the most beautiful thing you ever saw. I don't mean it's good for a house to be on fire, but bad things can be beautiful. I'm not a poetic guy, either, but maybe you could compare some fires to a dragon, like fire has different colors the way a dragon does, it keeps moving and changing, like I guess a dragon would, and sometimes you can get pretty close to it without really knowing it's there, and then all of a sudden it's huge in front of you and scares the shit out of you. It's my job to kill that dragon. When it lands on a building, I walk in there with an axe and a hose, and we're gonna stay there until one of us is a pile of black ashes. For ten years I've been a fireman in Cape May, New Jersey, right here where I was born and lived without a break. We've got a lot of old wooden houses here in Cape May, one of the things we're famous for, all those Victorian bed-and-breakfast places, but man, those wooden houses can burn the hell up in no time.

As a fireman, you run into some unusual things. I've seen a man stand naked outside a burning building, holding a TV, not even notice he wasn't wearing anything. I've watched people throw furniture out windows, I've seen fires that burned odd colors, like green, and I've run into buildings where bottles started to explode. I've had some weird experiences, just part of the job, but the weirdest thing I've run into in ten years was something I didn't even notice at first.

Back in April, early in the morning, we got called to a fire over on Kearney Avenue. It was a two-story place, nothing fancy, not one of the tourist places. We got the call early in the morning, around eight, and my shift hadn't even started. When we got there the fire was burning on the first floor. Of course the first thing you do is make sure people are out of the building. On one side of the house was a set of stairs going up the outside, so I ran up them to make sure there wasn't anybody up there. When I got almost to the top, the door up there opened and a woman came out, came running down the stairs. I had to stop and turn to the side to let her get by me. I asked if anybody else was up there, but she didn't answer, so I ran on up. I went through the whole upstairs and didn't see anybody, so I went back downstairs. Like I said, those wooden houses can burn up real damn fast, and even though we finally got the fire out, that house wasn't worth living in after the fire.

The next morning I was sitting in the firehouse, working on a crossword puzzle. I do a lot of crossword puzzles, wherever I am. So I'm sitting there and Chuck, my chief, comes in and asks me did I see the young woman who lived on the second floor at that house we were at yesterday. I say yeah, I saw her, she passed me on the stairs when I was going up.

"Did you?" he says. "You saw her? Cause nobody else's seen her since the fire."

"So what?" I say. I looked back down at 10 across, *The Invisible Man's* creator. "Her house burned up," I say. "She's staying with somebody."

"Yeah, maybe," Chuck says. "But her landlady and her sister haven't heard from her. You'd think if your house burned down you might call the landlord to find out about the damage. Or call your family to say you're alright. Her sister called asking if we saw her yesterday."

I stopped and looked up at Chuck. He had a point there. It was kind of an enigma when he described it like that. "Maybe she's been too upset to call," I say.

"Oh, yeah, right, Sherlock," Chuck says. "Just for the record, which way did she go when you saw her?"

"Down the stairs," I say. "I was headed up and I didn't look back at her. What's her name?"

"Marnia," he says, and went back to his office. I looked back down at my crossword puzzle and wrote HGWELLS in 10 across, but then I stopped to think about Marnia. I remembered her coming down the stairs, what she looked like. I could see her up above me running down, and she was perfectly alright when I saw her. So why didn't she call somebody? I sat there for a while thinking about that.

At noon I went up to the Captain's Cove to have lunch with my brother, Ben. Ben works on one of the fishing boats that come in across the street, over by the Lobster House. I can't imagine doing Ben's job, 'cause there's no goddamn way I'd get on one of those boats. I had a bad experience with the undertow when I was a kid, nearly drowned, and now I'm afraid of the water. When I think about all that water down under a fishing boat, sweet Jesus, I could nearly puke from fear of thinking about it. But Ben don't mind.

Ben was already waiting when I got to the restaurant, talking to Trina. She moved down here from north Jersey, and you can see Trina was real cute about twenty years ago. She ain't bad now, I mean, but twenty years ago, that was her time. "Did you order me some lunch?" I say to Ben.

"How the fuck do I know what you want?" he says. "I ordered you tuna salad."

33

"I hate tuna salad," I say.

Trina says, "You want a crab cake sandwich, fries, a small salad, and iced tea."

"How come she knows and you don't?" I say to Ben.

Trina brought our drinks and Ben says, "You get your tattoo yet?"

"I didn't say I'm definitely getting a tattoo," I say. "I'm thinking about it."

"Cheaper than a sports car," Ben says. "If you gotta have a middle-aged crisis."

"There's nobody middle-aged sitting at this table," I say.

"I don't know," Ben says. "Thirty-six." My little brother is still just twenty-nine.

"I got something to tell you," I say. "About the fire yesterday. Woman that lived on the top floor has sort of disappeared."

"What you mean sort of?" Ben says. "Like you can only see her in good light?"

"No, smartass," I say. "I mean both the landlady and her sister haven't heard from her, people you'd think she'd contact. If your house burned down, wouldn't you call me?"

"If my house burned down I guess you'd be standing there watching it."

"Alright, but you see my point."

"Yeah," Ben says. He reached up and took off his baseball cap and scratched his head. "Yeah, so what happened to her? Anybody die in the fire?"

"No. But here's what's fucking with my head. I saw her. She was coming down the stairs when I went up to check the house. She ran right by me, and I know she was OK, but now she's incognito."

Ben didn't say anything for a minute, then he says, "So she was there when the place caught fire. Maybe she set the fire."

"We already know how it started," I say. "Bad wiring downstairs, had nothing to do with her."

35

Ben says, "Huh. So what could have happened to her? She could've got kidnapped. She could've went down the street, I don't know, confused or something, and got murdered. She could've gone crazy and wandered off."

I stirred some sugar in my tea. I like it sweet. "Going crazy is the only one of them that makes sense," I say. "And even that don't make a lot of sense."

"So what if she just walked off," Ben says. "Not crazy, or not any crazier than the rest of us. What if she just said fuck it and walked off? I've had days I felt like that."

"Yeah, I've had a lot of them days," I say. "Maybe that's what she did."

When Trina brought our food out, I say, "Impeccable service."

"Yeah, hon," she says. "That's what we do here."

While we're eating, I say, "Would a person just walk off and leave all their stuff? I think I'd at least load my car."

36

"Maybe she didn't have a car," Ben says. "And how much stuff did she have?"

"Not too much after the fire," I say.

"So she abandoned her belongings that were piles of ashes. Big loss there. Maybe she had a boyfriend and they ran off," Ben says. "Took advantage of the opportunity."

"But she's a grown woman," I say. "She didn't need an excuse to leave. Maybe she was running from the law."

"Oh, there you go," Ben says. "Maybe she killed somebody and this fire was just a lucky break."

I was still thinking about Marnia when I got back to the firehouse. I asked Chuck what her last name was—Marnia DeMarco—and I called a buddy who's a cop, to see if he knew anything. Could be foul play or something. You never know till you find out. A couple of hours later, though, he called me back and said he couldn't find anything on her, not by that name and not by the description I gave him. I didn't really think he'd find anything, but now I knew. Maybe I should've forgot about it, but

I don't know, she went right by me, I could've reached out and touched her. Maybe I was the last person to see her. Anyway, I didn't forget about it.

That evening my girlfriend, Sharon, was coming over. I was making her dinner, and I wanted to talk to her about Marnia disappearing. I had to stop by the grocery store on the way. I don't understand how I can buy so little and it costs so much. Sometimes I walk out of there looking at my sales receipt thinking "What the fuck just happened?" While I was in the grocery store I saw a sort of pretty woman with straight red hair, young, early twenties, and for a second there I had a shock and thought it was Marnia. She could have been in the store. I mean she could have been, but she wasn't.

My girlfriend had a headache when she got to my house, so she wasn't much in a mood to talk about what was going on with my job, including Marnia. Lately, though, even when Sharon doesn't have a headache, she doesn't seem too interested in what I'm saying. But Sharon did say maybe Marnia ran away out of a sense of spite, telling everybody around her to drop dead. I guess that kind of went along with Ben's idea that Marnia said fuck it and left. But why would she want to tell everybody to drop dead? Was she on bad terms with every person she knew? Sharon's sister worked at Burdette Tomlin Hospital, over in Cape May Courthouse, and Sharon promised to call her to see if Marnia was there.

The next day Sharon called me at work. "Jen says they aren't supposed to give out information on patients," she says.

"Tell her this is an official investigation," I say.

"I don't need to," she says. "She told me anyway."

"Well for Christ's sake," I say, "why couldn't you just tell me that? So is Marnia in the hospital?"

"No."

After Sharon called, I called Marnia's landlord, who didn't know much. She says Marnia lived there about two years, was real quiet, and she worked at Cape May Whale Watcher, that takes tourists out to look at whales and dolphins. Sharon wanted to do that one time, and I told her if she had a gun she could shoot me, 'cause that was the only way I was going on a boat. This was probably the point where I should've said to hell with it, who knows where Marnia went, and got on back to my own dull life. Instead, I called Marnia's sister, said I wanted to come talk to her. Before I went to see her, though, I got in my pickup, which is getting old and needs replacing, which I don't even want to think about, and I drove up to the whale watch, right behind Captain's Cove, where I meet Ben for lunch. I talked to a couple of people there, who said Marnia didn't have a boyfriend, not that they knew about, she didn't seem to do much, she read a lot, and she seemed normal. I was thinking "What the fuck does 'normal' mean?" but there wasn't any point in asking. Marnia also left three CDs in the office there, and they gave them to me. One was some singer from Africa. The other two CDs were Patsy Cline, and I thought "Well, you go, Marnia." Anybody that likes old country music is after my heart, except I have a preference for George Jones, Merle Haggard, Marty

Robbins, those guys, the earlier stuff. But Patsy Cline, you can't go wrong there.

After the whale-watch place I drove out to see Marnia's sister Fanny, that lived across the Canal in Lower Township. Really there wasn't a whole lot Fanny could tell me either. She hadn't talked to Marnia in a month, and they weren't close, but she'd heard about the fire and when she didn't hear from Marnia, she started making calls.

"Even if we aren't real close, she's my sister, you know?" she says. "You hear your kid sister's house caught fire, you're gonna want to find out if she's OK. She should've called me by now. I'm real worried about her. If you hear anything, you let me know."

"Yeah, I sure will," I say.

I did find out from Fanny that her and Marnia grew up in Cape May, lived their whole lives there, hardly ever even went anywhere else. Join the club, I thought. She said Marnia had always kind of lived in her own world, whatever she meant by that.

When I put it all together, it wasn't much to put together. I didn't have any information to explain what happened to Marnia. Not sick, not killed, didn't seem like the desperate type. That evening I was sitting in my den having a beer, puzzling it out. I've got the den decorated up with an Old West motif, leather upholstery, cowboy paintings on the wall, a bar decorated with rope. It's my favorite room, reminds me of places I've never been, and I like to sit down there and read magazines, which is about all I read. I sat there drinking my beer, thinking, seeing Marnia coming down those stairs, trying to remember exactly what she looked like, what her expression was. Now I was trying to remember all the details of what I'd seen in her house upstairs. The main thing I remembered was that when I first went in, I was in a room that had a fishing net hanging above, covering the whole ceiling. And the whole room was filled with clear glass jars full of seashells, that she could've easy picked up on the beach. And what else was there? Yeah, a lot of potted plants. The room was kind of tropical in a way.

That night I had a dream that Marnia was talking to me. I could see her just a little, but I didn't know where she was. She said, "Why are you looking for me, Eli? You think you're gonna find me? I've had a nice day, though, went swimming." That was all I remembered, but it stuck with me the next morning.

Over the next week, no matter how much I thought about her, or talked to people, there were no clues, no ideas you could prove or not prove, it was just done. She was gone, disappeared after the fire, after I knew I saw her. Gone without a trace.

We got on into May, starting to have some pretty warm days, and the shoobies, the tourists, were back in town, filling up all the bed-and-breakfasts, going in all the little shops in the middle of town. I like the warm weather, but I don't care too much about the town getting so crowded. When the town really fills up, except for going to work, I tend to spend more time at my house, over in West Cape May. Even though it was weeks gone by, I kept thinking about the disappearing Marnia DeMarco. I had a feeling she was...I don't know, somewhere. I didn't have any doubt she was alive and well, but I couldn't figure out why somebody would just go away like that. Then while I was thinking about her I'd start to think "Maybe she did the right thing". I thought about leaving when I was younger, before I got on at the fire department. I've spent my whole life in Cape May, and sometimes I wonder if I'm gonna get old here and one day think "I never did anything and now it's too late". I'm thinking I need a trip, go out west maybe, Oklahoma or Montana. Maybe as soon as I buy a new truck. I ought to do that first.

Toward the end of May I was getting ready to go have lunch with Ben when Kenny, another one of the firemen, came in and says, "Take a look at this." He laid a photocopy of a newspaper article in front of me, and the headline read "Some Cape May Visitors Come From the Sky". I didn't see why I should care, but then I saw the name of the writer: Marnia DeMarco.

"My kid was doing research for class," Kenny says. "I took him to the library to look at old copies of the newspaper, and I got bored waiting on him, so I started looking at them. I'm going through and saw this name, and I thought, hey, that's the girl that disappeared."

"Son of a bitch," I say. "Thanks for bringing me this, Kenny." The article, which was about migratory birds, was from the *Cape May Star and Wave*. It was the kind of article they'll run here about once a year. At the bottom it said, "Marnia DeMarco is a writer who is native to Cape May." So she was a writer. I read the article, and it was pretty good, but I noticed it ended with saying something about how lucky migratory birds are to get to see the world. Maybe Marnia wanted an excursion of some kind too.

I dreamed about her again that night. The two of us were on a beach, looking out at the water, and she was asking me if I liked to fish. "You don't have to get in a boat," she said. "You can fish from shore." Then she spread out her arms, and they turned into wings, and she turned into a bird and flew off across the water.

Wherever she was, she was gone and nobody knew anything. Months went by, and at first I'd talk to her sister or the people at the whale-watch place and ask if they'd heard anything, but I finally gave up on that. In August I was sitting in the Mad Batter, where Sharon works, only she wasn't on that day. I was waiting for my buddy Lester to come have a beer with me, and while I was waiting I pulled out my crossword puzzle. What was 4 across, Spiritual leader? Nine letters, first letter D. I thought,"Deacon?" No, too short.

Then Lester came up and says, "So what's good?"

"You know something that's good?" I say. "Maybe I need to hear about it."

"A bar with air conditioning is the best thing I know," Lester says. Then he says, "Jill's gonna join us in a few minutes." Jill is Lester's wife.

"Long as she don't mind men drinking," I say. "Keeps life from being so dull," I say.

"You bored?" Lester asks me.

"Just the usual," I say. I don't tell him that I been thinking lately about getting my ear pierced.

Before we even saw the waitress again, Jill came up and Lester says, "Hey, hon," and when she sat down he's got to say, "Mr. Tikhonenko here was telling me about how boring his life is. Only thing exciting in Eli's life is looking for that girl that disappeared."

"At least you've touched on the truth," I say. "As usual, Lester exaggerates. But since I saw her come down those stairs I've thought a lot about her. You gotta admit it's mysterious."

"What did she look like?" Jill asks. I told her as best as I remembered, medium height, kind of thin, kind of pretty, straight red hair down to her shoulders. And she was wearing a light blue jacket.

"Well, that's strange," Jill says. "Maybe I saw her." Me and Lester stared at Jill like she was an alien.

"And you never told nobody?" Lester says.

"How was I supposed to know?" she says. "I never heard a description of her."

"It was in the paper."

"Not that part," Jill says.

"How do you know it was her?" I say.

"I don't, but I know I saw a woman a whole lot like that, red hair and light blue jacket."

"When did you see her?" I say.

"It was the day of the fire. I remember it cause that same day was my nephew's birthday, Robbie's, you remember, Lester."

"Isn't Robbie's birthday in February?" Lester says.

"Oh, good God, Lester. I was making a cake for his party. I had to go to the store because I ran out of candles."

"You sure about this?" I say.

"Yeah, I'm sure. People at the store were talking about the fire."

"But how do you know you saw Marnia?" I say.

"I don't really know that I did. I just know I saw a woman on Seashore Road, right before lunchtime, and she looked like the woman you described. I was driving real slow when I saw her 'cause somebody was turning."

"She does have a good memory for people," Lester says.

"My God," I say. "So you saw her the day of the fire."

"Maybe."

"Seashore Road," I say. "That's headed toward the ferry."

"That's possible," Lester says. "Maybe she took the ferry to Delaware."

"Well, where else did she go?" I say.

That evening I was sitting in my den, looking at a picture of a man getting bucked off a horse, and I knew Marnia walked to the ferry. She headed south, hitchhiked away, went to Florida maybe, caught a boat. I think she's somewhere down in the Caribbean now, laying on a beach, eating fish, sitting under palm trees. And she's doing just fine. I wish I was there with her.

Use My Blood

The man at the rest stop in Virginia offered us some peaches he had bought back in South Carolina. I took one for me and one for Meghann, and the man started telling me about the little town he's from in Maryland, a fishing village. I thought about how nice that would be, to live in a village on the coast, eat fresh fish off the boat. I could probably learn to like fish if I lived like that.

When we went back to our own picnic table, Meghann said, "You liked him, didn't you?"

"Yes, he seemed pretty nice," I told her.

"You don't know, Mom," Meghann said. "A stranger at a rest stop could be a psychopath."

Was my teenage daughter watching over my love life? "Well, we didn't set a date," I said. "He just gave us a couple of peaches."

"Maybe they're poisoned," Meghann said.

"Maybe," I replied, and bit into one of the most delicious peaches I thought I'd ever had. I sat there looking out at the pine trees and thinking back on the past week, on how unlikely it was that I was sitting there in Virginia with my daughter.

Friday: I was sitting at my desk looking at the list of blood-drive locations, seeing whether people wanted a bloodmobile or for us to set up inside the building. While I was doing this, Kristin, who wears too much eye makeup to be working for the Red Cross in my opinion, came by my desk.

"Sandy!" she said, "I just found out it's your birthday! I was just talking to LaRhonda and we said we wished we'd had time to plan something for you. But we should take you out to dinner."

I smiled at her because I try to be polite. "I'm not that big on birthdays," I said. "After a certain age they don't mean as much." Oh, maybe I wasn't truthful there. *After a certain age they mean even more,* is what I should have said. When you turn thirty-six you wince at every birthday that comes along, reminding you faster and faster just how much older you're getting, that your body isn't as good as it was, that if you're alone like I am, your chances are going down.

I don't really care much for Kristin, so I said I had plans for the evening, and instead of going out with people from work I came home to my house in Little Five Points. It's a cute house and I've fixed it up since Farlow and I bought it, and it needed some fixing up too, which is how we could afford it. That was a long time ago, though, before he left and we got divorced. Even now I miss him sometimes. I get angry at myself for feeling that way, because he sure doesn't deserve it.

When I got home that evening there was a package from my younger sister, Tabitha, who's studying modern politics in Montreal. It's a little hard to imagine, since I've never been to Montreal, and it seems so exotic to me. Tabitha and I haven't been talking as much lately, although we were very close when we were girls. She'd tell me about those incredible boyfriends she picked out, guys just enough above trash to be able to talk and drive. I looked at the package she had sent, small and wrapped in white paper, and took it in the house. It hadn't occurred to me that Tabitha would even remember it was my birthday. I looked at Tabitha's handwriting on the package, with my name and address lettered out in purple: Sandy Stillwater, 270 Josephine Street, Atlanta, Georgia, 30307 United States.

What was inside was as good as I'd hoped. Tabitha had sent me a pair of green cloisonné earrings, utterly beautiful, in a woven Celtic motif, and I knew she had really thought about what I'd like. She doesn't care about the fact that we're Irish, doesn't even really believe it. Mom's mother was the only one of our grandparents who was from Ireland, and because Tabitha hates Mom she denies even that connection. But when she picked out these earrings Tabitha remembered that I care about our Irish background.

I was taking myself out to dinner, and I tried on three outfits hoping for something that matched the earrings, but nothing was really right. I knew I'd need to buy a new blouse to go with the earrings, but I found something in the meantime that would at least do for the evening. When I looked at myself in the mirror I wondered how much it showed that I was a year older. I wish I was prettier; it would be easier to age if I was prettier. I'm afraid I will not get better looking as I get older, and men do not want a woman who is growing less attractive. Am I going to wind up living alone? I think about that. My chin is a little too small, set back too much so you can see this soft flesh underneath, and I've got too many teeth, so they kind of push forward, which isn't good with my thin face. At least I have beautiful eyes, they're my best feature. I've been told I'm pretty by several men, but even if everything about me was right, which it isn't, I'm too pale, no real color, so I have to depend on makeup not to look like a ghost. My hair is plain, just regular straight brown like so many people have, but I do like the way it's cut, the way it curves up at the ends.

I walked down to Little Five Points thinking about birthdays. Why do we celebrate them when all they do is remind us of getting older? And I didn't really have anyone to celebrate with. Of course I wasn't entirely alone until a week ago, when my daughter, Meghann, moved out. She's fourteen, a child, and she moved out. Actually she moved in with a friend, for the last two weeks of school, but still. I talked with Meghann's friend's mom, who agreed to let Meghann stay with them till school was out. I shouldn't have agreed, but my God I needed the break. That little baby girl that I held in my arms, that I fed and kept alive from my own breast, that I dressed up cute to take her out, who'd come running to see me with a smile so beautiful I almost cried from happiness, that same child screamed at me that I'm the stupidest mother in America. But I love her. When Shakespeare had Lady Macbeth say that she would pull a baby away from her breast and kill it, I wonder if even Shakespeare understood how evil that is. Did he know how twisted a woman's soul would have to be to pull a baby away from her breast and kill it? One of the best memories I have is looking down and seeing Meghann suckling at my breast, her eyes barely open.

Saturday: Will African violets really bloom all year round? I've been told they will, but mine don't, so I don't know if that's true. I was sitting in my enclosed porch Saturday morning, looking at the four African violets I have on a glass table there, and the pink one was blooming. I was looking at the other plants and thinking *aren't you happy there?* I keep an old toy fire engine on the shelf below the violets. I know I'm just torturing myself keeping that toy there, looking at it and reliving all the memories it brings back, but I can't get rid of it. I was sitting there drinking a cup of tea, wearing my green house robe and reading the newspaper, when the phone rang.

"Hello," I said, lowering the paper and picking up the phone.

"Sandy, this is Farlow." My ex-husband calling. Why was he calling on a Saturday morning? He doesn't call me to chat.

"Hello, Farlow."

"Sandy, I just got a call from Meghann." I closed my eyes and was glad he couldn't see my face. Frowning makes me ugly.

"Yeah, she's staying with a friend," I said. Oh, maybe I wasn't truthful there. *She's escaped from the mother she can't stand to be around* is what I should have said.

"She made it sound like she's moved out completely and moved in with another family."

"It's a temporary arrangement. We needed some space from each other."

"*Space*? I never heard of anybody having space from their own kid."

"Well, it happens. I think it's better for both of us for a while, and it's only a couple of weeks until school is out. She wanted to stay with her friend Willa, and I've talked to Willa's mom. It's OK." Why couldn't Farlow just call to say something nice to me once in a while? Why couldn't he do that? Did he even know it was my birthday yesterday?

"Maybe you're right about having space. It doesn't seem like things are working out with her staying there. I'm thinking she should come live with me."

"No, she's staying here," I said. "People have problems, but they work them out. We agreed that she would live with me."

"Well that doesn't seem to be happening."

"I don't know what she told you, Farlow, but this is temporary."

"You know, you've had problems with her before. Maybe she would be better off over here for a while. We've got to think about Meghann's best interests."

"I think about her all day long," I said. "Are you doing that? Remember calling her two days *after* her birthday?"

After Farlow finally left my phone alone my hands were shaking. I tried to drink more of my tea, but it was cold and bitter. Even if Meghann was running away at the moment, it hadn't always been like that. I felt agitated after the phone call and couldn't sit still. I got up and walked around in the house, then decided to go out and ride my bike. Out on the bike path I passed an older woman and her grown daughter, holding hands. I wondered if I ever held hands with my mother. Not that I would want to. And when I thought about it, when was the last time I held hands with anyone? Then I remembered the earrings from my sister, the trouble she had taken to pick out something she knew I'd really like, and I wanted to hold her hand.

There have been times when Tabitha and I were really close. I remember sitting up late at night as girls, talking with a flashlight, making scary faces by shining the light up our noses and giggling, being shouted at by our father from another room to go to sleep. Tabitha and I played together a lot when we were young. I remember one occasion, though, when I didn't want to be bothered with her. I was fourteen then, and my nine-year-old sister wanted me to play a game with her, but I wanted to go to the dock at the lake and lie in the sun. Even while she was still begging me to play, I ignored her and headed for the lake, so she tagged along. That hot sun was so relaxing, and the rough wooden boards of the dock made a nice texture against my skin. I was lying there thinking about how perfect a tan I could get when I heard a splash. I sat up quickly and heard a wet and gurgled scream. My little sister had fallen off the end of the dock. Then I shouted, "Dad! Dad! Dad! Dad!" looking around frantically for help. Thank God he came running. I was stupidly helpless, a memory that embarrasses me at the same time that I'm sickened to remember my father pulling Tabitha out already unconscious.

That's a bad memory, but Tabitha is OK, studying modern politics in Montreal. The memory of Tabitha almost drowning doesn't bother me so much because of what happened to her. She's OK. I try hard to avoid that memory because of where it leads, but sometimes a dark wave sweeps me along anyway, and there's Tabitha coming up unconscious out of the water. And then I see the body of my son, Patrick, after he drowned.

Six years ago I was sitting out on the porch on a warm fall day, cracking pecans. Patrick was five, and I had said he could go play with a friend from kindergarten, so the friend's mother had driven over to get him for a few hours. Kids are worse than cats in their curiosity. How can you possibly keep them safe when in only ten minutes they can go out the back door, pull back the cover of an aboveground pool to look for dead bugs, then fall in and drown? Patrick's friend ran to get his mother, but half an hour later a policeman was walking up the sidewalk to my porch, where I still sat with a lap full of pecan shells. As soon as I looked up and saw the serious face of that young officer, I felt like I would throw up and my arms grew weak, dropping down into my lap on the rough shells. After Patrick died it left a hole at the bottom of my soul, a place where the darkness never goes away.

Maybe because I was thinking about Patrick that he came to me that evening. It had started raining and I was listening to a Beatles CD, so I heard the rain outside along with the words John Lennon was singing from Lady Madonna. Maybe I sang along a little bit myself, but then the words I expected didn't come. Instead I heard John Lennon's voice say, "Mama" and I thought *What? I don't remember that on this CD.* I stopped and stood there. The music had stopped, and all I heard was the rain. Then it was my son's voice saying, "Mama, it's me, Patrick."

"Patrick?" I said.

"I'm OK," he told me.

"Patrick baby," I said.

"It's OK here."

"OK where?"

"It's all nice people here," he said. "It's not bad."

"Patrick, where are you? Are you really talking to me?"

"Yes, I am."

"I love you baby," I said.

"I love you too, Mama."

That was all he said, then John Lennon was singing again, and the room got blurry because my eyes filled up with tears.

Sunday: Go to church, close your eyes, and what do you see? There is an ocean inside of me, right in the middle, and when I close my eyes and concentrate I can get away from the world and go swimming there in that warm blue water. Sometimes I do that to escape, but other times I do it just for the pleasure of being there. I was raised Episcopalian from my father's side, and even though I have Irish blood, once in a while I go to a service. After Patrick came to me Saturday night I wanted some spiritual connection, so I went. I enjoyed the ritual and familiar feeling of the service, and while the preacher was talking I found that I closed my eyes and went down inside to that peaceful ocean.

When I got home I sat on the porch in my wicker chair and read an article about the band Blondie, with a picture of the band. It struck me how beautiful Debbie Harry was and I thought, *Well, that's what a nice photo touchup will do for you, she must be, what? in her forties?* Then the article said she's fifty-three, and I couldn't believe it. What would it be like if you always left everyone breathless with how beautiful you are? How could you ever be sure how they felt about you, the real person inside the body? No matter what we look like, there's a person in there. Sometimes down in Little Five Points I see a tiny old woman, she looks Chinese to me, who always wears a chartreuse cap and sits on a bench in the square. It's almost like she doesn't exist, but I think, *This is a human being, just like me, and maybe she's sitting there remembering a man she loved back in China, remembering the feel of his hands on her body, or she's thinking about God and whether we have a soul.* Of course our bodies are not important to our value as human beings. I wish I was a little prettier, though.

I laid the paper down and thought about who I am inside. Even if the body isn't important, I think I have a woman's soul.

It's just who I am, and I can't imagine anything else. That means I can give birth and be a mother, and love my children.

Monday: There was a staff blood drive on Monday. I like it when we encourage people who work at headquarters to give blood. Since I spend so much time trying to arrange for people to give, I like the idea that the people I work with are part of that. And I like giving blood myself, the idea of giving life from my body. There's a part in the process where you have two bar-code stickers on a piece of paper; beside one is the label "Use my blood" and beside the other is "Don't use my blood". While you're sitting there alone after your blood is drawn, you have to pick one and put it on your paperwork. It gives you a chance to have private second thoughts, to say whether you think your blood is safe to give to other people. I like that feeling of choosing, of saying I want to help someone. I always say to use my blood.

That evening when I came home I had a message from Lila, who I don't see very often, asking if I wanted to go to a movie. Lila and I like to talk about gardening, planting and flowers, and trading hosta. I knew I should do something with Lila, since it had been a while, so I called her back and we agreed to go to dinner. I went to take a shower, and after I got dressed I saw another message on the phone. I figured Lila must have called, but when I checked, it wasn't Lila. It was Farlow. He'd left a message telling me that he'd talked to a lawyer that day. He said he hadn't actually done anything legally, just talked to the lawyer for information. "We should be able to talk about this," he said, "just talk it out as Meghann's parents and decide what's best for her." Since Farlow had already decided, I wondered what it was he thought we should talk about.

I was really upset when I saw Lila, but it was good that I had a chance to talk to her. I'd have been worse if I had just sat around the house brooding and angry at Farlow. Sometimes we need to talk to someone, even if all they do is sit there and nod.

Sometimes all we want them to do is sit there and nod. Men don't understand that. They always want to fix it, but you can't throw your spear at every problem. Lila let me talk, and I wound up telling her about funny things Meghann did as a little girl. I was even laughing when I described how when Meghann was four years old, she got ahold of some lipstick and did the makeup for another little girl. It wasn't all that funny when it happened, but it is now. By the end of the evening I felt better. But I still had to deal with Farlow.

Wednesday: And in the evening on Wednesday I went after work to a once-a-month women's discussion group that meets at different people's houses, where we talk about our lives and issues that we're having. It was at Wendy's house, and only five of us were there, I guess because of the bad rain. Whenever it rains I always abandon fashion and wear an old pair of lace-up waterproof boots that I've had for years. They're not cute, but they keep my feet dry, so I waded up the sidewalk in my boots. I also wore a hat because of the rain. It would be nice to wear a hat more often, except they never look very good on me. I like the way hats look on other people, but when I put one on, I usually just look like I'm trying to look weird.

During the evening I went to the bathroom, which Wendy had decorated with a wall of framed photographs of people. The bathroom is a strange place for photographs, I've got to admit, but it sort of worked. One photograph really caught my eye, in a bright yellow frame. It showed two children sitting on a couch, about four and two years old. The older child was looking right at the camera and laughing, a free open laugh that looked like total pleasure and joy. I never saw a child look happier than that. I stood there in that green-and-yellow bathroom for a long time and looked at that picture, and I started to think about Patrick, until I felt heavy.

He came to me again after I got home. I was in the kitchen thinking about having a glass of wine. It was quiet in the house and pat pat pat the rain was hitting the windows. Then inside the sound of the rain I heard Patrick, a small wet voice, say, "Mama, it's me."

"How are you, baby," I asked.

"I'm OK, Mama," he said. "Really I am."

"I want to believe you," I said. "But I miss you."

"You're too sad, Mama," he said.

I listened a long time more, but he didn't say anything else. And I knew I was too sad.

Thursday: Be melancholy once in a while; it adds depth and complexity to the soul. Don't be as melancholy as me, though. I've decided that I'm too moody. I spent most of the day thinking about my little girl, wondering what to do and feeling a little helpless. Just another week until school was out, and then what? Would Farlow drive to Atlanta to try to take her back? Would she go? The more I thought about her the more I wanted to talk to her, and in the afternoon when I thought she would be home I called over to Willa's house and asked for her.

"Hello," Meghann said, very neutral, not friendly or glad to hear from me, but at least not angry or negative.

"Hey," I said. "I just wondered how you're getting along."

"OK."

"Do you need anything from the house? Can I bring you anything?"

"No, I'm OK."

"How was school today?"

"Boring. I missed first period." She knew that telling me about first period would set me off, since getting to school late so often had caused some of our biggest fights. But I let it go.

"Well, I was missing you," I said. "Just wanted to see if you're alright."

"Yeah, I'm OK."

Did it mean anything to her that I called? I felt irritated and a little depressed when I got off the phone.

Just before I sat down to eat supper that night Farlow called again. "I talked some more to the lawyer," he said. "I don't think it should come to this, but she thinks I have grounds to ask for custody. I don't want to do that. I just want us to talk and agree for Meghann to come live with me for a while."

I sat down feeling a little sick to my stomach listening to him. "Farlow," I said, and I hoped I sounded firm instead of shaky and upset, the way I felt, "you and I made an agreement. Whatever problems you and I had, I thought I could trust you."

"Sandy, I don't think that's even fair. I'm not trying to do anything dishonest."

"I won't let you take away my daughter," I said. I think I sounded firm on that.

"She's my daughter, too. I have a right to think about her."

"Then think about her. You know I've always been close to Meghann. You used to comment on it. So now I've got some difficulty with her. I'm not the first person who had problems with their teenaged kid. People work it out."

"Look, maybe not permanently," he said. "But she'd be better off here for a while at least."

So I didn't eat dinner. I walked into and out of every room in the house, several times, just wearing my bathrobe. I went to the dining room and wondered why I was there, then remembered I hadn't eaten, then I went to Meghann's room, then my room. Back and forth, in and out of the rooms. Back and forth. Meghann's room. My room. What was I going to do? Could he do this? In and out of the rooms.

Saturday: Happy people are all alike as far as I'm concerned. It's the unhappy people who seem different. Actually, there aren't that many happy people, but the few you meet all blur together. The people who really stick in your head, who really strike you, are the most unhappy ones. You wonder how they bear their miseries, what little bits of joy they find to keep dragging themselves through the world. They're interesting, and I'm tired of being interesting. Or I'm not all that interesting either, but I'm tired of being unhappy.

I didn't sleep Friday night, awake until six a.m., lying there thinking, if you could call that cyclone in my head thinking. Then I fell asleep until eleven. When I woke up, I realized I had just been dreaming about my sister. While I was still lying there half awake, I thought about Tabitha up in Montreal, imagined her in her apartment, walking down the street, buying coffee.

In the afternoon I was walking in the park, tired from lack of sleep, but feeling too jumpy to sit in my house. I was thinking about what Farlow might do, wondering whether Meghann would even agree with him, wondering what I should do. Then an idea started to come to me, and I could feel my heart beat faster from excitement.

At lunch time I called and asked to talk to Meghann.

"Yeah?"

"Hi, honey," I said.

"Hi."

"I was thinking. You've always wanted to go see the Statue of Liberty."

"Yeah?" she said. She sounded a little suspicious.

"Yeah, I was thinking we could drive up to New York."

"When?" She had the usual uninterested tone of voice. But then she surprised me. "Yeah, I'd like to see it." She sounded more enthusiastic.

Now I surprised her. "I know yall don't really do that much during the last week of school," I said. "So I thought we might leave Monday."

"OK, sure," she said. Now she definitely sounded enthusiastic. No argument from Meghann about skipping school.

"Yeah, this'll be fun," I said.

"How come we're doing this now?"

"I've got time off from work. And this seems like a good time to go. I better get to packing, though, and do some things. Anything in particular you want me to pack for you?"

"I'll come over tomorrow and do it," she said.

"OK, then I'll see you tomorrow."

I hung up feeling scared. I'd admit that to anybody. Except Farlow maybe. Or Meghann. But what kind of life is it if you don't do things because you're scared?

I finished eating the South Carolina peach and went to the restroom to wash off the juice. When I came back I saw Meghann sitting on the picnic table, watching some kids walk their dog. I think Meghann would like a dog. I'll talk to my sister about what would be a good kind up there. When we get to New York, I'll tell Meghann that since we're so close, we can go on up to Montreal to see her aunt. And if we need to, we'll keep going. Because nobody is going to make me lose my child. Maybe some kind of Husky would be a good dog.

The Smallest Dreams in the City

Anton must have been drunk, because he was laughing. He boarded upstairs in the old house where my family lived, but my mama didn't know he drank whiskey when I was around him. She had no idea. Maybe she figured tiny men were different from regular men. He was telling me about religion that cold afternoon. "You know, Lilly," he said, "there was a man back where I came from—" he came from the town of Tuckasegee, North Carolina "—who ran a pool hall, but he wanted to be a preacher. You know what a pool hall is?"

I said yes. I guess Anton thought seven-year-old girls never heard of pool, but my papa drove a truck long distance, and when he was home in Asheville, he loved to play pool.

"Do you? So he ran a pool hall and sold beer, but he couldn't forget about preaching. Guess his mother raised him right. And he wouldn't let anybody cuss while they played pool—you know what cussing is?"

I said yes.

"Do you? Well, don't that beat damn all?" Anton laughed some more. "Couldn't cuss while you played pool. Nobody ever played worth a damn with a hen-pick rule like that. Except my brother. He played pretty good pool. If you said 'Praise Jesus!' whenever you drank your beer, then once in a while the preacher would give you a free beer. Praise Jesus! There sure was a lot of praising Jesus, but you know what, Lilly?"

I said no.

Anton took another drink from his green bottle, then said, "That guy was only fooling himself, that preacher. Nobody meant it. They only said 'Praise Jesus' to get free beer. Oh yeah, free beer. Praise Jesus." At the time it didn't occur to me that Anton was not one of the men playing pool. What little I knew about pool, I figured Anton was a pool player, too, but it's hard to play pool when you only stand three feet, six inches tall.

Anton never said he was drinking whiskey when I was with him. Whatever he drank from those glass bottles, he always called it "the deacon's fruit juice". I asked that day for a drink of it.

"No, Lilly," he said. "This juice isn't for little girls. Only grown men can drink this." He took a swig, then said, "Well, I guess a few exceptions. I drink it, too."

"Did the deacon make it?" I asked. I really wanted to drink from that green bottle.

"No, honey, the deacon couldn't make deer's ears or dog's daisies. He just sells it. Like at the store."

"What kind of juice is it?" I reached over and snapped off a leaf from the potted violet on the windowsill. Anton lined his sills with violets, so the windows were filled with dark green, pink, and purple.

"What kind of—honey, don't pull those leaves off. That's my dog violet."

"Dog violet?"

Many years later I was remembering that afternoon with the snow drifting down on Montford Avenue outside, me sitting on a little chair that went with the tiny kitchen table. A lot of Anton's furniture was small, just for him. I must have been one of the few guests who could use his furniture. In fact, I don't know that he ever had any other guests. That's how I was remembering that afternoon, and suddenly I remembered that my mama, I don't know when, years later, said they had arrested Deacon Wallace from the First Baptist Church.

"Don't worry about the juice," Anton said that snowy afternoon. "I'll get you a Coke and tell you a story. You want it in a glass?"

"No."

"OK. Well, you know that big church out on Wolfe Avenue?"

"No."

"No? Well, it's there. Big white church with a tall steeple and columns in front. We had a church looked sort of like that back in Sylva, near where I lived—"

"What's a dog violet?" I asked again.

"Now hush, and listen to the story..."

Twilit snow fell softly, darkly on Christmas Eve, as the sky settled to sleep on the ground. Turning his face to the cold, blue snow, Wood Winston, tall, thin, red-eyed, stood in front of the church in downtown Sylva. He scratched his unwashed head through the holes in his stocking cap, shifted about in his worn plaid jacket and listened to the distant sound of singing from inside the church, like angels off on the other side of Heaven. The contented worshippers inside the warm church, who he had seen going in, were dressed in special new Christmas garments, the bright reds of our Lord and green of the Holy Ghost. What a glorious time to celebrate. Just think of it.

Standing out on the sidewalk, Wood did not think of our Lord, but looked down instead and remembered the sweltering day three years before when cats had lain panting in doorways, when old men coming into town had sat forlornly in the barbershop, too hot to tell lies, and when Wood had helped build the frame for pouring this sidewalk. He could still see that cement, now hardened and hidden under the snow, slopping onto the ground in the shimmering summer haze. He drank five Dr. Peppers that day before noon, and ate half his lunch, giving the other half to the mangy white street dog. He looked around again in the darkness of December. The angelic singing seemed louder.

Wood turned away from the lighted church and continued down the darkened street, snowflakes striking him softly in the face like chilled fairy kisses. This street ran past the clothing stores, the Italian restaurant, the theater that had been closed for years. It rolled on past auto-parts stores where teenagers congregated at night, past the high school on the hill overlooking the supermarket, and on through the hills into the Tuckasegee Valley, winding up the mountain toward Cashiers. Three days ago Wood had been in Cashiers with a vague cough, hands scratched and red with cold, cutting and stacking the last-minute Christmas trees from the farms in the mountains. But Wood was not thinking now of Christmas trees lying in stacked bundles crunchy with ice, nor of our Lord; he was thinking of a ham sandwich he'd had yesterday, of how good it was and of how he'd like another. It had mustard on it. A pickle was on the side.

The alleluias from the church grew suddenly louder, and so clear and sweet that Wood turned in surprise. He once knew a girl who sang sweet high alleluias like that. The dark sky over the church grew brighter and a gentle light, soft as a cotton gown, opened a hole in the sky like a night flower. With cries ringing like bells, a thousand angels came pouring through the light, singing songs in a language no human tongue had ever pronounced. As Wood watched in open-mouthed astonishment, his hunger disappeared, his head grew lighter and a burning sensation spread across his shoulder blades. Then he felt himself rising off the ground. He glanced behind to see two white wings flashing in the night, lifting him into God's choir.

The preacher in the church halted in mid-sentence (he had just said "lovely baby Jesus") the instant the church

windows flashed with the light of Paradise. The church grew
hushed as a cathedral, then swelled with the aerial sound of the
sky choir. The faces of the amazed worshippers looked about for
the source of the music. Could it be a miracle, those faces asked,
something to test our faith? The roof of the church disappeared
as the thousand angels flew down into the open sanctuary, their
wings brushing softly against the walls. Every worshipper—from
the preacher and deacons (car salesmen and supermarket
managers) to conservative gray women with large red bows
pinned to their breasts, young women with curled hair and
freshly ironed white blouses, and young men standing stiffly in
dark suits—every worshipper stared with awe and wonder and
amazement at the bright host singing above them.

It was a miracle.

Then they noticed him. He hovered in front of the bright
host, beating his wings slowly, looking slightly confused, still
wearing the red and brown plaid jacket and ragged stocking cap.
Once they realized he was there, the congregation looked only at

Wood and ignored the angels. Seeing Wood floating up there, turning his head from side to side in a perplexed way, where only purity and beauty should be, the preacher grew angry. "Wood!" he cried. "What are you doing up there?" The whole miracle was being spoiled. The preacher wanted to cry. "He's ruining it!" he exclaimed.

Other people realized that the preacher was right, that the beautiful pageant, this gift from Heaven, was being diminished by the presence of Wood Winston. "He doesn't belong there!" some said, scowling, while others asked indignantly, "Why is he doing this?" Finally, an elderly woman at the back, wearing an attractive gray dress with black trim and a single strand of pearls, said, "I don't have to be insulted this way." She got up stiffly and left. A young couple then rose, the husband staring angrily up at Wood, the pretty wife shaking her head, bouncing her curly hair. More people left, until the discontented preacher himself marched toward the exit. In a few minutes the church was totally empty, other than Wood Winston and the thousand angels.

The choir continued to sing, Wood had no idea for how long, but at some point he found himself sitting alone in the dark quiet church. In his hand was a ham sandwich. He bit into it and thought he had never had one so good. It had mustard on it. A pickle lay on the pew beside him.

Anton was a singer. I guess it's how he made his living, or no, I'm sure it's how he made his living. It's the only thing I ever knew he did. He'd been singing a long time, and he said once that when he was a child he wanted to sing in the movies. "Can you see me in the movies?" he asked. "I could be Roy Rogers' sidekick. When he started singing I could climb up on the fence and say, 'Howdy, Roy,' and sing a duet with him." Instead of singing in the movies, Anton sang in the church choir back in Tuckasegee. His mother had wanted him to be a church choir director. He told me that, but he only mentioned his mother that one time that I can remember. I asked where his mother lived, but he just said, "That's enough on that subject," and wouldn't talk about her any more.

He sang in a club when I knew him, or maybe in several clubs, in Asheville. Sometimes he sang me children's songs, "Old MacDonald" or "While Away the Hours". Once he asked if I'd like to hear a special song, then he got up to stand by the window. It was getting dark out and he looked like another child, like me, standing there by the window, until he started singing in that low voice he had. He sang a song that was popular then. I'd heard it on the radio, called "She Has Eyes That Make the Angels Cry". I was about eight years old then, so I couldn't appreciate everything about the song, but I remember it now, the few minutes that he sang, all these years later. While he sang, the breeze blew a smell of lilac in the window, and when he stopped singing he turned around, and I saw that he was crying.

A couple of months later we were in the park when a pretty woman walked by. She towered over us (and I was by then already taller than Anton). He stopped and lifted his hat. "Good afternoon, Sue Jean," he said.

"Well, hello, Anton," she replied. "I'm sorry I didn't get to see you after you sang the other night. Larry had a headache and we had to leave early, but I wanted to thank you for inviting me. I've never heard singing so beautiful. And that song, what was it, 'OK by Me'?"

"'It's Alright With Me.' Darrel Porter. I'm glad you enjoyed it. Maybe you'll come back some time."

"Maybe I will. Maybe I'll come without Larry. I'm serious, I never heard such a lovely voice. You have the sweetest singing I ever heard."

Sue Jean went on and Anton stood staring after her so long that I finally said, "Are we gonna get the ice cream?"

Anton turned to me and said, "Do you know that woman?"

"No."

"That's Sue Jean Wallace. You know Deacon Wallace?"

"The deacon's fruit juice?" I said.

"That's right, the deacon's special fruit juice. And that's the deacon's special daughter." Anton stopped walking and said, "If you stop growing now, Lilly, then when you get older I'll take you dancing. Do you like to dance?"

"I sure do!" I said and leaped around lively to show him.

He looked back down the way we'd come and said, "Sue Jean's a little tall for me to dance with."

After we'd bought our ice cream, we sat on a park bench while Anton told me what the different kinds of birds were. A blue jay flew by screeching and he said, "You know how to recognize the call of a blue jay? They make a noise like a rusty pump handle."

"What's a pump handle?" I asked.

"Lilly," he said, "you city children don't know deer's ears or dog's daisies about the world." He listened again as the jay creaked. "What's a pump handle... I wouldn't really want you to stop growing, Lilly. I hope you grow up to be tall and beautiful like Sue Jean."

"I don't want to grow up," I said.

"Well, some ways you're right, but mostly you're wrong. Do you want a story? It's about a woman with your name."

"Named Lilly?"

"That's right, named Lilly..."

If you could fly along the valley, rising on the warm currents above the river and between the hills, if when the mountain rose up at the end you could then soar up the mountainside, skimming along above the trees, you'd come eventually to a small house, high up the mountain. The house has a streaked and rusted tin roof and is made of weathered unpainted boards, with a small crumbling porch on the front. A garden once lay in back, a neat garden with a tiny fence, potatoes in hills, and beans climbing tall poles. The garden is all weedy now, with trees growing in it.

In the front yard is a giant oak tree, 150 years old, gnarled and majestic, but split by a bolt of lightning. This is the house Lilly lived in.

Lilly was born long ago, so long ago before grandfathers were children that young people could not imagine such a time. When she met the Devil, Lilly was already an old woman who had lived alone all her life. One day Lilly was sitting on her porch on the front of the house when a young man rode up on a bright chestnut horse.

"Good afternoon," the young man said. "Am I anywhere near the Barron place?"

Even though she was old, Lilly nearly gasped from delight. She had never seen a man so beautiful. He had soft brown eyes with long lashes, dark curly hair and a gentle smile. "You're near it," she said. "On up the road to the next place."

"Finally," he said and wiped his brow. "I've eaten my pound of dust today. You suppose I could get a drink of water?"

"Dipper's on the well, yonder on the side." Lilly watched closely as he dismounted and walked around to the well. What was happening to her, she wondered. How could a young man have this effect on an old woman who had already heard the creak of Heaven's gate opening for her? He walked back around to his proud horse a minute later, thanked her with the most charming voice she'd ever heard, and rode off.

After he was gone, Lilly sat dreaming. When she remembered his soft eyes and sweet smile, she felt like a young girl, wanting to put her hands on his face, caress his smooth skin, and kiss him. The dream faded as she heard the cawing of crows chasing away a hawk. Reality came down, like a great tree falling, and crushed her. Lilly rose, slowly and stiffly, went into her little house, lay down on her bed, and began to cry.

Why had she spent her life alone?

Why did her blood begin to run warm now, to surge with the hotness of life, when she was too old to use such emotions? Lilly's tears were as bitter as lye.

"So don't just cry about it," she heard a man's voice say. She looked up sharply and saw a pleasant-looking man with white hair and a ruddy face, dressed in clean blue overalls with shining brass buttons, sitting at her table. "Don't just lie there crying about it," the man said again. "You want that young man? His name is Levon, by the way. I'll arrange it."

"Who are you?" Lilly asked, sitting up. "What are you doing in my house?"

The man laughed and a gold tooth caught the light. "I'm here to do you a favor. I've had a good day. There's been a lot of wickedness in the world today. I'm in the mood to do somebody a favor, and you're the first one I found. You want to be young? You want Levon to fall in love with you? I'm offering it. Take it or leave it."

"I'll take it," Lilly said quickly. "What do you want?"

The pleasant stranger grinned broadly. "Nothing. Just enjoy it." Lilly felt a flush, a hot wave, rushing over her. She was light-headed for a moment, and when the swirl of air and light cleared, the man was gone. Something felt odd about her body. She then realized with amazement—all the aches and pains she had known for years were gone. She leaped up, lighter and faster than she thought she ever had, to look in the mirror. A cry of terror, of joy, of incredulity passed her soft red lips as she looked at the beautiful girl in the mirror. The beautiful girl in the mirror.

Days later, Lilly lay beside Levon, astonished that something so wonderful had finally happened to her. Her heart was beating like the pulse of the center of the earth as she squeezed her arms around him. Her lips brushed his cheek, a hundred soft little kisses, and he wrapped his arms tighter around her.

Lilly and Levon were married in August, when days were hot and mountain nights were cool, when the flowers in Lilly's garden were lush and blue and high, and apples sagged the branches of the apple trees. As fall came on, with early frosts and poplar trees turning yellow, Lilly and Levon lay late in the mornings, warm under Lilly's sawtooth-star quilts. In winter the snow fell deep on their mountain, where they told one another tales in their warm house. Levon powdered the snow with wood chips as he split logs all winter for the stove while Lilly baked biscuits and an occasional fruit pie. A very happy year went by, and Lilly's previous life, alone and growing old, seemed a strange and unpleasant dream that she was glad to have woken up from. Now she lived as she was meant to live, loving and being loved.

Small flowers in pale pinks and yellows rolled as a blanket over the meadows in the spring. In the summer, black and white cows ate grass in those same meadows, where thistle grew like witches' fists in the fall, and everything slept as seeds through the winter. On and on this cycle continued, flowers, grass, thistles, seeds, as years passed. Sometimes there were thistles between Lilly and Levon, disagreements and arguments, but the thistles were never allowed to grow. Lilly sewed shirts for Levon, and he built her a swing under the huge oak tree. Sometimes he called her Diamond Lil, and in the mornings he would kiss her on the neck to wake her. Occasionally in the evenings, Levon talked about people he'd known growing up down in Georgia, and Lilly would laugh until she got the hiccups. Then Levon would start laughing.

As the years passed, Levon's curly dark hair lightened like snow, his pretty face growing more like a winter field, full of furrows and unspoken knowledge. One night Lilly came into the bedroom where Levon lay sleeping. She carried a candle and stopped to look at him lying there. She wanted to bend down and kiss him, to wake him, but instead she walked over to a mirror hanging on the wall and looked in it. Staring solemnly back at her, with sad serious eyes, was the same beautiful young girl who had married Levon so many years ago. Lilly had feared it for some time now—she was not aging along with Levon.

Many years later Levon died, an old man. A misery-stricken young girl threw herself on his grave, clutching handfuls of the earth, moaning and crying. No one had ever seen such intense grief at a funeral. Later that day, Lilly sat in her house, her eyes red, her mouth grim, her fingers still covered with soil from Levon's grave. She felt she would never smile again. As she sat there, she looked up slowly to see a white-haired, ruddy-faced man in overalls grinning at her. "So why are you crying?" he asked. "Didn't I give you what you wanted? I made you young."

"You made my husband die."

"Of course I didn't. I don't have that power. He died a natural death."

"But you could have stopped it. I'm still young, and for what?"

"Well, yes." The Devil laughed, his gold tooth flashing. "I admit I tricked you. Having a little fun. On the one hand I gave you what you wanted, but on the other hand you can never win when you make a deal with me." He chuckled in a low voice. "Whatever you do, you lose."

Lilly stared at him hard, then rose from the table and turned away. She caught sight of the wide straw hat, hanging on the stand Levon had made. It was the hat she wore when they walked down to the creek together. She then looked over at the bed where they had lain together so many nights. Everywhere she looked in this house, Levon was there. She turned slowly back to the Devil and said, "Lose? You think I lost? I was an old woman dying. Never so much as been kissed. Never had a man look up glad to see me. But because of you I spent a whole lifetime with a man who loved me, and I loved him. Even if he's gone now, you can't change that. I had something you'll never have no matter how many people you fool. I had somebody to love me." Lilly stared at the Devil. "And you think I lost?"

The Devil looked at Lilly a moment in dismay, then a dark anger like the lunge of a snake came over his face. With a hiss of cold wind, he left the house, and out in the yard Lilly heard a burst of thunder so loud a front window cracked. She ran to the door and saw that a bolt of lightning had just split the oak tree in front of the house. As she stood there, she felt a stiffness and heaviness coming over her. Slowly she walked to the mirror. When she looked in, an old woman smiled sadly back at her.

The last time I saw Anton, I was nine years old, and I believed that I was growing up, as one of the boys at school had asked me that afternoon to be his girlfriend. I got home from school that day just before it started to rain, a hard driving rain with scary loud thunder. I went and put my schoolbooks away, then came into the foyer, where Anton was wearing his green rubber raincoat. I intended to sit in the big stuffed chair with King George stripes on it. That's what my papa called it, but I still don't know what he meant. I had a book with me, to curl up and read, and Anton was looking out the glass door at the rain.

"What do the bigger birds do in this weather?" he asked. Then he saw that I had climbed into the chair with my book, and he said, "What are you reading?"

"Treasure Island," I said.

He leaned over, pulled the hood of his raincoat over his head, closed his eyes, waved his arms around and shouted, "Find 'em, boys, find 'em! Get the money!" Then he straightened up and asked, "Who is that?"

"I don't know," I said.

"Why, it's Blind Pew," he said. I think he was a little disappointed that I didn't know, but I told him that I hadn't read the book yet. "Well, I'm sure you'll like it," he told me, then he looked out the door again. "I sure don't want to go out in this cruel, wet world. But I guess I'd better. See you later, Lilly." I was already reading the first page when he left. I read for half an hour and decided that the book was too difficult. So I never finished it and still don't know who Blind Pew is.

The next afternoon, a sunny Saturday, I was with my mama in the kitchen making cookies. That same Saturday afternoon Anton met the deacon's daughter, Sue Jean, at the hotel downtown. Sue Jean was with Anton on the fifth floor of the hotel when her husband, Larry, kicked the door in. I saw a picture of Larry later in the newspaper. He had a sort of square face and wore his hair in a flat-top. I thought at the time that he looked like a Marine. He had a mean expression. My papa went to school with Larry, and years later, when Larry got out of prison, my papa said that Larry wasn't really mean, but that he was "so dumb if he'd been a caveman, he wouldn't have known how to use a rock". At his trial, Larry said that when he kicked in the door, Sue Jean was lying on the bed with her blouse open and Anton was "feeling her up". The newspapers said that. My papa read it out loud to my mama, and then he noticed that I had come into the room. Of course Sue Jean said that she and Anton were just sitting there talking. Those things don't really matter, though. What matters is that the window was open and that Larry ran across the room, grabbed Anton, and threw him out the window.

I believe now that when Anton's body went out the window, his soul continued on across the city, looking down on Asheville, surrounded by green mountains, the rivers flashing in

102

the sun. I believe his soul went singing across those mountains, dancing away into the blue sky, telling tales of the Appalachian Mountains.

But his body? Oh Lord. It fell five stories from the hotel window and shattered onto the sidewalk. I found out about Anton's death when someone called my mama that afternoon and told her. She came back into the kitchen, where I was helping her bake cookies, with a real mad expression on her face. "What is it, Mama?" I asked. "Mama, what happened?"

"What makes you think something happened?" she said, then set a bowl down on the counter so hard it broke.

I started crying. "What happened?" I said again.

My mama and papa helped dispose of Anton's belongings, since no one wanted them. His family couldn't be found, and no friends turned up. Everything he had was gotten rid of, except for the pots of violets that sat on his windowsills. There were about thirty of them, blooming in pink and purple and blue. My mama kept them, and over the years we would occasionally break a leaf off one and root it, to start a new plant. Until last week I had a pink violet descended from Anton's plant. It was sitting on the computer desk. It was the last of those violets, but when I came home after a weekend trip, I found that my cat had knocked the pot off the desk, and the broken leaves had lain for two days in the sun and wilted. I cried for an hour when I found it. At first I felt foolish crying so much over a plant, but I know what it really was. I was crying for Anton. I think I'm the only person who ever cried for him, the only person who ever really cared that that lonely man had lived.

A Night at the Carnival

When she had first looked at the apartment she'd noticed a bar across the street where college kids were sitting at tables on the sidewalk. It occurred to her for a few seconds that they would be there at night, that they could get noisy, but then she opened to door to the living room closet. So much space! She had looked out the kitchen window at the green trees of a park, and perhaps the sight of the greenery reminded her that unlike her current tiny place, this apartment didn't smell of cigarette smoke. She had turned to the landlord and asked how much the deposit was. He asked for $200, and she pulled out cash. That same evening, visiting her mother and sitting in her living room, listening to her mother complain about people at the church, wishing her mother would just be silent for a few minutes, it suddenly occurred to Toni again that the apartment might be noisy. That could explain why it was only $400 a month. But she had paid the deposit, and if she didn't take the place she would lose the money. She couldn't really afford to lose $200 while she was living on her small savings.

She turned over now in bed and heard the noise from the street coming to her as if she were sitting down there at a table. "Hey, Patel!" a student yelled from the street below Toni's apartment. "Where the fuck you been?" Another voice yelled, "Studying micro! Did you drink up all the beer?"

Toni looked over at the clock and saw that it was two in the morning. Why hadn't she just given up the $200 deposit? But this was how she always seemed to do things, as if she were running blind into the darkness. She sat up, feeling frustrated, and sighed loudly. At least the cigarette-smelling apartment had been quiet. Out of the frying pan... After a few minutes of sitting in bed, listening to noise from across the street, she decided to get dressed and go for a walk. Toni generally was a little frightened to be out at night alone, but she felt like she needed to get out of her apartment, and it was a warm June night. She would be OK.

Walking through the darkness toward a residential neighborhood, she thought about rent being due in three days, which reminded her that she needed to find work, at least something part-time. Her needs weren't great, but she had stayed in town longer than she expected. When she had moved back to Pennsylvania to live with her mother—temporarily, she thought, only for six months, then definitely back to Providence—she'd discovered how much her mother still drove her crazy. At eighteen it had been daring and romantic for Toni to move away from her mother, to swim out into the great stream of life's possibilities. At forty-five, moving back in felt like wading waist-deep through a swamp that stretched in all directions, and Toni was soon scrambling to find her own apartment, however small.

Probably the very reason Toni had moved to town could have been more clearly spelled out, but of course, impulsiveness and vague plans, this was Toni's way. How often had she wondered how she got to where she was? Yet when her mother asked for help composing a history of the family, writing up family stories, and including old photographs, Toni felt flattered and moved back to State College. That brief period had now lasted more than a year, as Toni floundered in passivity. In addition to the book, there was also a plan, maybe, to clear out the garage, so jammed with junk that no car had gone into that building in ten years.

Farther down the street where she was walking after leaving her apartment, she saw the bright light of a small diner. As she got closer, she saw what a charmless place it was, a one-story rectangle, partly red brick, partly brown aluminum siding, with a single large window filled with hand-lettered notices proclaiming various menu items. *Apple pie like Mom.* There were no cars parked nearby, but through the window she could see people inside.

"Missy! Missy!" A slightly nasal voice on her right caused Toni to turn. A woman wearing a long, flower-print skirt and a ragged green sweater, in spite of the warm summer night, was standing on the sidewalk several feet from Toni. "Hey, missy," the woman said again. "You got a quarter? I'm only asking for a quarter. Maybe I can get something to eat."

"You won't be able to buy much with a quarter," Toni said.

"Just a quarter," the woman said. "That's twenty-five cents. I'm only asking for twenty-five cents."

"Are you hungry?" Toni asked.

"Yeah, missy. I haven't eaten all day. I used to teach college at the academy, and now I'm hungry."

This ragged woman with hair that needed washing didn't look like she had ever taught anywhere. "Do you want a sandwich?" Toni decided that the woman must be about her own age, in her mid-forties. *I could wind up like that,* she thought, wallowing for a moment in the horror of the idea.

"Yeah, I like sandwiches. Except sardines. I hate sardines. You know they got the eyes in 'em."

Toni didn't like sardines either, but from what she remembered, canned sardines didn't have the heads, so they couldn't have eyes. "Let's go in," she told the woman. "I'll buy you a sandwich."

"Oh, you're a Christian, missy. Unless you're Jewish, but you seem Christian." The woman turned with Toni to enter Maddie's Diner. As they pushed open the door to go in, the woman said, "My name is Adele."

"I'm Toni. Do you live around here?"

"No, I live near the Hastings people. Near the pumpkin farm. You know where the pumpkin farm is."

"I'm not from around here," Toni said, wondering how true this was. She had grown up here. "I never heard of the pumpkin farm." They sat down in a booth, and now that she was there, Toni wondered whether the woman was really stable enough to sit with.

"Oh, yeah, the pumpkin farm," Adele said. She turned toward the one woman working behind the counter, who was pouring coffee for a man sitting there. "Hey!" Adele yelled loudly. "Hey! We're trying to order something here!"

Toni frowned at the outburst and hoped that the waitress wouldn't associate her with that behavior. But of course she would. They were sitting together.

"I'll get to you," the woman behind the counter said, glaring at them.

The man who was getting coffee turned around. Adele looked at him, then asked loudly, "You know where the pumpkin farm is?"

"Yeah," he said. "Most people know that."

Adele looked back at Toni. "What'd I tell you?" she said. "Pumpkins."

A moment later the waitress came over, not looking friendly, and said, "What can I get you?"

"Tuna salad sandwich," Adele said. "You ever put cheese on it?"

"Of course we put cheese on it. It's called a tuna melt."

"Oh yeah, yeah. I remember them. I'll have a tuna melt."

The waitress turned to Toni. "I'll just have a cup of coffee," Toni said. "You have decaf?"

"Yeah." The waitress turned away from them.

Adele leaned over the table toward Toni and said breathily, in a loud whisper, "Don't give her a good tip. This service isn't very good."

"I think she's irritated that you yelled at her," Toni said.

Adele sat back and looked surprised. "That's no reason for bad service. Jeez, if everybody acted like that just because you yelled at them…"

"I wouldn't like it if somebody yelled at me," Toni said. "I bet you wouldn't like it either."

"People yelled at me all my life," Adele said. "I got used to it."

"I'm sorry you did," Toni said. They sat without speaking for a few minutes, and the silence felt awkward to Toni. She wasn't sure how to talk to Adele, and felt uncomfortable that she had asked her in. She wondered how rude it would seem to simply pay for the food and leave. It was early morning, and she could say she needed to get home. Adele was rolling her napkin into a tube, unrolling it, then rolling it up again.

Suddenly Adele laid the napkin aside and said, "So you're not from here?" She didn't seem upset at all.

"I was born here," Toni said, "but I haven't lived here almost thirty years."

"Oh." Adele was staring at her and nodding seriously. "This is your street?"

"No," Toni answered, and wondered how much she wanted to tell her. "I don't think I've ever been on this street. I think I got a little lost."

"It's easy to get lost," Adele said. "Maybe I'm lost right now." She sighed and looked a little melancholy for a moment. "I can't always tell."

Toni sighed softly. What could she say? "Can you find your way home?" she asked.

Adele seemed to brighten up a bit. "Oh, I don't want to go home anyway. Do you want to hear a story about my mother? Her name is Sissy."

"That's an unusual name."

"Yeah, that's her name." Adele laughed. "You don't meet many Sissys."

"I never met any."

"So this story is about getting lost. It happened to Sissy when she was a little girl."

Toni didn't believe this was about Adele's mother. Though what difference did it make really? "You call your mother by her first name?" she said.

"I always did," Adele said. "I didn't like to admit she was my mother. So when Sissy was a little girl, she was raised by Aunt Gail and Uncle Raymond. They weren't really her aunt and uncle, but they took her in because Sissy's real mother left her with them and went away."

"That must have been bad for Sissy," Toni said.

"It must have been. So here's the story. One time when Sissy was little, Aunt Gail and Uncle Raymond said they would take her to the carnival." Adele stopped and turned around toward the counter. "Where's my tuna melt?" she said. "I hope it's not Swiss cheese." She turned back. "Sissy wasn't the kind of little girl who cried much. She learned not to do that."

"How old was she?" Toni asked. "I mean when she went to the carnival."

"I heard she was eight. It was in the fall and the carnival came to town. Not this town, another one, where they lived. Sissy and Aunt Gail and Uncle Raymond lived out in the country in a big wooden house, but the carnival was more in town. One evening after supper they got in the car and drove back toward town, to the fairgrounds where the carnival was set up. Uncle Raymond was driving because he was smoking a cigar. He had a mustache. This was in the fall, but it wasn't cold, so Sissy just had on a dress. Aunt Gail told Sissy she could have a dollar to spend any way she wanted. They were nice to Sissy, even if she couldn't have friends come over to the house. Aunt Gail even used to put flowers in Sissy's room. So Uncle Raymond bought tickets to get into the carnival, and the first thing they did was go to look at the sheep show. Sissy didn't like sheep, because she didn't like the way they smelled, but she was just a little girl, so she had to go along. They went in and looked at sheep for a while, and Sissy was choking from the smell of the sheep. It didn't bother a lot of people, but Sissy was walking around holding her hand on her nose. Uncle Raymond would—oh hey!"

Adele stopped the story as the waitress came over and set down a plate with a sandwich on it. For Toni she put down a cup of coffee, then she turned to Adele.

"You want anything to drink?"

"No," Adele said. The waitress shrugged and turned.

"It's cheddar," Adele said happily. "That's my favorite cheese. Do you like cheddar?"

"I don't eat cheese," Toni said. "I'm a vegan."

"A what? A vegetarian? Why can't you eat cheese?"

"I can eat cheese. I used to eat it, but I'm a vegan. That means I don't eat anything from animals." The thought ran through Toni's mind—for the five hundredth time?—that she should print up cards explaining what a vegan is, so she could just hand them to people and not have to explain this over and over, answer the same incredulous questions about eggs, cheese, milk, yes goddamn it, even unfertilized eggs.

"I don't see what's wrong with animals," Adele said and took a bite of her sandwich.

"There's nothing wrong with animals," Toni told her. "I think the animals would prefer it if we didn't eat them."

"I'm pretty sure they don't kill cows when they make cheese," Adele replied. Toni felt tired, as it must be around three in the morning, and she didn't want to respond to that, so she

117

waited, but Adele didn't follow it up. Toni added sugar to her coffee, but no milk, and took a sip. She was surprised how good it was, not too strong and not bitter.

They sat while Adele ate her sandwich. She ate more delicately than Toni had expected, taking small bites and chewing slowly. Toni drank her coffee and began to think about a conversation with her mother that afternoon, about whether to include family recipes in the family history. *What we ate is part of our history,* her mother had said. Toni had pretended not to hear her and had kept typing.

When Adele finished the sandwich, she sat for a moment, then without looking at Toni said, "Sissy got tired of the smell of the sheep, and she was glad when it looked like Uncle Raymond and Aunt Gail were ready to leave the pens. They walked toward the door and Sissy was hurrying to get out. Then Uncle Raymond met somebody he knew and stopped, but Sissy went on outside to get fresh air. She stood out there a minute until she saw Aunt Gail come out. Aunt Gail was wearing a dress with big orange flowers on it, and she started walking away, so Sissy followed her. Then Aunt Gail turned the corner and Sissy saw that it wasn't Aunt Gail, just a woman who had on a dress that looked like hers. Sissy was surprised—you can figure that out, I'm sure—and she turned around and went back, and even went inside, but Aunt Gail and Uncle Raymond were gone. That's when Sissy realized she was lost. She was just eight years old, and she was lost at the carnival."

After a moment of silence, Toni said, "How long did it take her to find them?"

"A long time," Adele answered. "Hours. I don't know. A long time. She got scared and started walking back the way they came in, back toward the car, but she got mixed up. It was a big carnival, easy to get lost there, just like other places. She said she passed by booths where people were throwing things to win prizes, laughing and having fun, and men were working there yelling for people to come play. One of 'em yelled at Sissy and said 'Hey little girl, where's your daddy?' Sissy didn't even know where Uncle Raymond was, and she didn't have any idea where her daddy might be. Can you imagine that?" Adele leaned over the table and looked at Toni.

"I can imagine it," Toni said. "It makes Sissy's life sound hard."

"It probably was. She was lost at the carnival, and a man was yelling at her. For a while she was scared, then she saw people riding on rides and she liked that. They were going round and round in those things, the whatchamacallums, you know what I mean? They make you puke. Sissy said she stood there for a while watching people go round, and then she got hungry and remembered that Aunt Gail gave her a dollar. She found the food area and bought herself a hot dog, then some kettle corn, then a lemonade. After she ate she felt a little happier, and she saw another ride that went high up in the air. She walked toward it, but then she got even more lost. It was darker where she was walking, and the people were talking so she couldn't understand them, maybe a foreign language of some kind." Adele stopped for a moment, said, "Foreign." She pushed one last crust of bread around on her plate, then continued. "Sissy thought there were a lot of people talking that way she couldn't understand, and she sure wasn't happy now. Now she was more scared, because she couldn't even tell anybody that she was lost. After those people went away she saw a fat man, fatter than anybody she ever saw. He was walking really slow, you know how they walk, kind of side to side." Adele stopped talking, puffed out her cheeks as if she were fat, and leaned slowly to the left, then slowly to the right, then back again.

"And Sissy said he was breathing really hard, like he couldn't catch a breath. She liked his hat because it was red, she told me that, but the worst thing, the worst thing was that the fat man saw Sissy, and he asked if she could help him. She didn't know what kind of help he wanted. She was only eight years old, how could she help that fat man? He was fat and she was only eight years old. She turned around and ran away from him, around a building, and it seemed pretty dark there. She heard the noises from the carnival, but it seemed like a long way off. Sissy was so scared now she felt like crying. That's what she said. I'm not making this up. And I told you she was the kind of girl who didn't cry much, didn't I? But now she wanted to. Then she saw a woman in a long white dress, like an angel's dress, all the way down to the ground. The woman saw Sissy and said 'Little girl, you want me to tell your fortune? You want to know the future, little girl?' Sissy didn't want to know the future, and she ran away, just like she did from the fat man." Adele stopped and nodded, as if satisfied with Sissy's decision to run.

"I wouldn't want to know the future either," Adele said. "Would you?"

"No," Toni said. "I'm pretty sure I wouldn't want to know."

"When Sissy stopped running she heard a growl and looked over and saw a bear."

"They had animals at the carnival?" Toni said.

"I guess they did. I don't think it was a wild bear. But it must have escaped, because it wasn't in a cage."

"I don't know if I can believe this," Toni said. "A bear just walking around loose? Not hurting anybody?"

"Well, it wasn't walking around," Adele told her. "It was hurt, so it couldn't walk. It was sitting in one place. It was moaning, like bear-crying." She stopped speaking and made a low growly noise, but with an element of pain mixed in, imitating what she must have imagined the bear sounded like. "Grrrrowwwww. Sissy saw the bear, but instead of being scared, she felt sorry for it."

Now Toni said to hell with it, and decided to play along. "So she bandaged the bear's paw?" she asked.

"Good God, no!" Adele answered. "Even a little girl like Sissy knew not to walk up to a bear. And anyway, she wasn't a veterinarian. She just looked at the bear for a minute and kept walking. She was trying to get back to the main part of the carnival, but she had gotten really lost and didn't know where she was. She saw a lot of odd things."

"Yeah, you could say that," Toni said.

"I am saying that. But she said the strangest thing she saw, or the most scary, was two clowns fighting. They had big clown noses, and clown hair like this—" Adele put both hands on top of her head, with her fingers in the air. "And they were fighting, knocking each other down. When she saw that, Sissy took off running, it didn't matter which way. But then she got lucky, because she saw a woman in a dress with orange flowers, and this time it was Aunt Gail. Aunt Gail and Uncle Raymond had been looking all over the carnival for Sissy, and they had the police looking. When they found her, they went home."

Toni closed her eyes a moment, realizing how tired she felt. "It's an interesting story," she said to Adele, "but I think I need to go back. I'm really tired."

"Yeah, yeah," Adele said. "I've got somewhere I've got to be."

That sounded unlikely at this time of night, but Toni just replied, "OK."

"Thanks for the sandwich," Adele said.

"You're welcome," Toni said. Then she asked, "Can you get home OK?"

"Yeah, I'm OK." Was it just Toni's tired imagination, or did Adele sound slightly angry? She said again, "I've got somewhere I've got to go."

Outside the diner, Toni turned back the way she had come, but stopping to watch Adele walk off into the darkness without looking back. Toni went back along the dark streets, and as she got closer to downtown, she passed three young people. She assumed they were students, as they were all Chinese, talking with animation, and she listened to the rising and falling tones of the language as they passed.

And then she saw her apartment building. She was glad to see it, but when she got closer, two young men, probably from the bar across the street and thoroughly drunk, were in the parking lot, facing off, talking loudly, and shoving their palms against one another's chests.

"Come on and start something!" one of them slurred to the other. "I'll finish it for you."

Toni sighed and went around them, then into her building. As she lay down in bed again, she was grateful that it was now quiet across the street. What a strange night. At last she drifted off to sleep again, to dream of bright lights and cotton candy, searching for a woman in a flowered dress.

Everyone's a Winner Here

Like a brain fever is what it is, like a dumb murderous dream turned into chemicals in the blood. Somewhere in the body, maybe in the medulla oblongata, maybe in a corner of the adrenal glands, cells of hope exude the pernicious protein of belief, secrete that polypeptide of faith. The eyes grow brighter, the fist clenches in affirmation, the breath pushes faster out into the hot, sticky air, and the brain knows that this time winning is certain.

The chemicals of dreaming flowed like a river in the summer of 2005, like whirlpools and undercurrents in the blood of Jack, Francis, Darrel, and Anthony. Jack, Francis, and Anthony are what we call "white" men, since trivial things are important. We call Darrel a "black" man, or "African American" in the summer of 2005. These four men, college roommates from Rutgers, have dreams burning in their blood. Jack will pay for their room in Atlantic City, then act like the expense was of no consequence. *"No es nada,"* he says. No big deal. All he needs in return is to impress the hell out of everyone around him, the only thing he really wants out of life. This plan won't work with Darrel, because Darrel doesn't admire anybody he knows personally. He admires Charlie Parker, David Sanborn, Coleman Hawkins. Saxophone men. Darrel plans to play that sax right on into the Marines. Anthony needs to lay his fingers on those chips at the gambling table, feel the rush when the wheel spins. Earn enough money, maybe he'll drop out of college, go to seminary. Be a priest. If he wins in Atlantic City, that will be God speaking, won't it? And Francis, ah Francis. What's he doing here? He's trying to avoid dealing with a fight he had with his girlfriend. Doesn't want to think about it. He's driving, that's what he's doing.

Eighty miles an hour down the Atlantic City Expressway, past the endless forests and blueberry fields. "What the fuck is this?" Jack says. Lights ahead, SUVs sitting, gagging the blueberry fields with exhaust. "Ah, come on, goddamnit! It's not even moving." Jack's magnanimous plan is not supposed to start with sitting in traffic. Atlantic City Expressway jammed immobile, sullen creeping, loud sighs.

"I told you guys we needed to leave earlier," Francis says. "It's always like this in the summer. Everybody's going to the shore." The fifth cigarette on this drive slips between his lips, lighter snaps. *Thank God, nicotine.*

Add an angry hour, and if you don't like it, what are you going to do about it? Every ten minutes curse the cars, curse the fat dumbass in the black Toyota, curse the stupid bitch who lets too much room get between her and the car in front. Close to Atlantic City, the green boredom of the trees finally stops and some real life starts. Billboards tell you what you're about to get: sex, lots of easy money, and all the happiness you can cram in your pockets and in your mouth. Believe that dream, because you really are different from every pathetic schlump who ever dragged their middle-class ass to town.

"Alright, we're finally here," Darrel says. "I'm in serious need of some relaxation. The world owes me some Atlantic City candy." Straight ahead, red letters as tall as a mobile home, TRUMP PLAZA. Down Missouri Avenue, then left on Pacific. Here it is, the mecca of desperate dreams and entertainment through repetitious losing. From the corner, the name TRUMP can be seen seven times on the Plaza, the anxious, existential cries of a little man who secretly knows his value to the world.

"Let's get our ass parked," says Anthony. "I got money that needs a brother. Jesus let it happen."

"Jesus got nothing to do with it," Jack says.

"Let me drive down the street a couple of blocks," says Francis. "I want to see the place. I never been here. This place looks crazy." They drive by Caesars, fountain out front, four giant white horses with golden hooves and harnesses. In a chariot behind the horses is a snow white Roman, could be Julius himself, wearing a gold vest, bright red cape flying behind him, like an ancient Superman. A Muslim woman is walking past the statue, all in black, only the eyes showing. Wild West Casino has a wild west scenario, fake rocks, fake cacti, real seagulls flying overhead. Bally's palace of sex, easy money, and imitation delight looks all glass and chrome, and one corner of the building is rounded, like the torch from the Statue of Liberty. Several overweight Hispanics are on the corner, waiting on the bus. Across the street is the Frank Sinatra wing of the Atlantic City Medical Center. So party! The Frank Sinatra wing of the Atlantic City Medical Center is just across the street.

Francis is worried where he's going to park, but hark and behold, the ancient Romans have built a parking garage next to Caesars. Francis pulls in, turns a corner, and suddenly slams on the brakes. Screeches. Nearly hits a man in a wheelchair. Angel of Death flies away, cheated. The hysterical bitch pushing the wheelchair pounds her fist on Francis's window.

"Hey, I'm sorry!" Francis yells through the window. "I didn't see him! I'm sorry! I'm really sorry!" He backs up, goes around them, and drives off too quickly, squeals the tires.

"Way to go, dude," Jack says. "You nearly creamed that guy. We could've had a dead cripple on our hands."

Francis is shaking now, hoping the woman doesn't call the police or somebody.

From the garage, a glass-enclosed bridge above the street leads to the hotel-casino. The syringe of glass injects the frantic drug of gamblers into the casino. All along the edges of the garage stand a legion of Julius Caesar statues, all with one arm out, all pointing at the casino. What are they saying? *There is where you will have such fun.* Jack, Darrel, Francis, and Anthony go to the hotel desk, just off the Forum, to check in. Their room is on the tenth floor, across the Forum, past an even-larger statue of Julius Caesar, with dates of birth and death. A happy young woman poses in front of it, waiting for her boyfriend to photograph her for eternity with the giant plaster statue.

In the room at last, Francis flops onto the bed. He's thinking about the woman pounding on the car window. He's thinking about his girlfriend. He needs a cigarette. He needs a drink.

132

"Don't sleep now," Jack says. "We're here. Should've slept on the way over."

"I was driving," Francis says. "I'm not on vacation all the time."

"Too bad for you," Jack says.

Darrel pulls out a twenty, picture of Andrew Jackson, seventh president, father of the Cherokee gulag. "Twenty-dollar baby," Darrel says to the killer president. He holds the bill up to his ear. "What's that? You say you want to gamble? You bet you do, motherfucker." Darrel's eyes glitter and he moves his fingers as though he is holding his saxophone.

As these boys walk through the casino, beams of light enter their eyes, the photons strike the retina, hop on that electrical signal up the optic nerve into the brain. Thin tubes of nerves running up and down and crisscrossing, then crisscrossing again, millions and millions, firing out the chemicals of neurotransmitters to drift across the synapses. There's the blue glow of glutamate, there the gold sparkle of serotonin. So much potential in here. Some people might use all this activity and come up with a new way to teach kids to read. Or they might discover how to eradicate fire ants. They might create a new recipe with anchovies and potatoes. Of course all that brain activity might result in this: *Why doesn't that ugly old broad brush her hair before she goes out in public?* (that's Darrel); *Oh sweet fucking Jesus, look at the ass on that chick* (that's Jack); *How can these old people afford to lose so much money?* (that's Francis); *Concentrate, man, just concentrate* (that's Anthony).

And there's table games, and there's Keno, and there's TV betting on horses, and in the great palace of small dreams on the first floor, slot machines and slot machines and slot machines. "I'm going for blackjack," Anthony says.

"You know how to play that?" Jack asks. "You want me to give you some pointers?"

"No, I'm good at blackjack. My dad taught me."

"Think you're going to get lucky?"

"No, it's not luck. I know how to play."

"Well, I plan to get lucky myself, later," Jack says. Plans to be a dentist. Never worries about tuition. Plans to get lucky.

Anthony sits at the table. Black chick is dealing, Fatima on her name tag, here at multinational Caesars. Lot of dealers here have hopeful dreams of their own to make a life in America: Fatima, Jagat and Hung and Chan, dealing cards, moving chips, watching the customers. Men in suits are standing nearby, watching Fatima, Jagat and Hung and Chan. Between deals, Anthony pushes out a hundred-dollar bill. Fatima gives him twenty red five-dollar chips, then begins to deal the cards. *Alright,* he thinks *concentrate. Don't screw this up, that's not even a possibility.* He quickly crosses himself. *Please help me, God,* he prays and touches a finger to his chest over his heart for good luck.

Jack, Darrel, and Francis go down to the ninth circle below. A great hall is filled with slot machines, which ring periodically and perpetually. So many machines are going at once that the air is filled with a constant ringing din, as though the music of the spheres has suddenly gotten louder. The boys take seats at the slot machines to watch the twirling images spinning in front of them. Win. Lose. Win. Lose. Lose. Lose. Win. Win. Win. Win. Win. Ring. Ring. Music of the spheres, baby. The sound waves bounce into the ear, through the eardrum, across the teeny bones, then round and round the fluid canals and back up a nerve into the brain again. The electricity in there is flashing like the lights in a city. Red streamers of dopamine are going off like flares. Darrel is thinking *Keep it coming, just keep it coming, I feel my fingers on that new saxophone.* Francis is thinking *What difference does it make now? I'm going when the semester is over. I signed the paper.* Jack is thinking *Where's that waitress? Get your ass over here, puta, I need a drink.* Two hours later, $50 up for Darrel, $40 up for Francis, $60 up for Jack.

"Yall hungry?" Darrel asks. "I could kill some food."

"Yeah, I could eat," says Francis. He pulls the arm on the slot machine again, but doesn't even watch to see how it comes up, doesn't expect to win. "You guys want to take a break?"

Anthony won't leave the blackjack table. "I'm winning here," he says. "I've won a thousand dollars." Huh. Maybe he really does know how to play. Or maybe God is helping him cheat. He did, after all, ask for divine intercession. "You guys go on. I'll get something later."

In the restaurant, while they wait for the food to come, Francis says, "She should've brought the beers already. I could really use a beer." He knows he can't smoke in here, but the beer would be a welcome drug.

Jack sits back in his chair, says, "I got a special treat, *compadres.*"

"Yeah?" says Darrel. "What you got?"

"I got a phone number to call for hookers, the kind that work the hotels. I'll buy us some dessert."

Darrel brightens up. "High-class whores. I could get into that. I could get deep into that."

Jack turns to Francis. "How about you? You want some *mujer*?"

"Uh, I don't know," Francis says, and immediately his girlfriend comes to mind. "I wasn't thinking about it."

"Better slide on in while you can get it," Jack says. "You won't get much pussy in Iraq."

"Well, I'm in," Darrel says. "Count me in for the whores."

"Not whores. Don't talk like a peasant. These are call girls."

"Yeah, whatever," Darrel says. He moves his hand in the air, fingers curled together, in imaginary masturbation.

Tina and Desiree. Tina is from Atlantic City, twenty-two years old, very thin, with short blond hair. Desiree is from South Carolina, twenty-four years old, but in New Jersey since she was twelve, when her father moved the family. She's a little plump, with reddish-brown hair. Tina wants to be a dental assistant. Desiree has no ambitions except to deaden the pain.

At the blackjack table downstairs, Anthony has started to lose. First you win, then you lose. Unless you lose and then you lose. That's God's plan for most of us. Down to $900. That's OK. Then down to $700. Not OK, but it's tolerable. Anthony makes his bet. Down to $400. Angrily, he shoves his chips out. $200. With a cold heart and trying not to panic, more chips out. $50 left.

Darrel goes downstairs to give Anthony the glad tidings that young whores are in the hotel room. On the way, he passes a statue of an old guy in a toga, Marcus Tullius, it says. Whoever. He sees copies of famous statues, old dead white guys, that's all he knows. The penises broken off in antiquity have been generously restored. The pendulous genitalia hurry him on to his task.

Tomorrow, when Francis asks, Darrel will say that Anthony looked "intense". Darrel sits down on a seat next to Anthony at the blackjack table, and Anthony turns to him with his intense look.

"How you making out, Grand Master?" Darrel asks.

Anthony glances over at Darrel, doesn't say anything. Almost like he doesn't know him, still not talking, then he leans over and says softly, "I kinda got a problem."

"What kind of problem?" Darrel asks. He frowns. He doesn't want to hear about a problem. He doesn't even want to know about anybody else's problems.

"Yeah, um, I'm sort of losing. I was doing so good. I won a thousand."

"But now you're losing it?"

"Jesus Christ, man," Anthony says. "I'm this close to losing it. I took $500 from my dad's store, and it's gone. He doesn't know I took it."

"What about the thousand?"

"It's fucking gone, you understand?" Oops, public display of anguish. People are looking. Anthony grinds his voice down low. "And the five hundred is gone. This is fucked up. Man, this is fucked up. It's like, I mean, I was winning." Darrel sees Anthony's hands shaking. "Can you loan me some money?" Anthony asks.

"Yeah." Darrel's voice is flat. "Yeah, sure. I didn't bring much down." He looks in his pocket. $50. "That's it," he says.

"OK." Anthony takes it. He turns back to the table.

"Oh, hey," Darrel says. "I came down to tell you. There's a couple of hookers in the room."

"Yeah, OK. You guys have a good time." Anthony has already pushed the fifty across to Fatima and is watching her brown fingers count each chip.

The radio is playing "Born to Run" when Darrel comes back to the room. Tina is dancing. Darrel stands in front of her and starts dancing, too. Jack is preparing beautiful little rows of fine white powder. Snow-white beauty. "You girls got lucky," Jack says. "You can get fucked up before you get fucked. You can show me how grateful you are after you get high."

"Yeah, baby," Desiree says. She puts an arm around Jack's waist and wetly kisses him on the neck, runs a hand across his chest. Everybody in the room takes a snort of the cocaine. Oohhhhh yeah! Tina gives a long kiss to Darrel, tongue like a snake, her hand moving down his stomach, stops just short of his cock and grins at him. She stands up and begins to dance more. She looks at Darrel as she dances, then unbuttons her blouse and takes it off. She sits down on his lap, facing him, still moving to the music, and pulls off her bra. She puts one hand behind his head and pulls his face down onto her breasts. Francis is sitting on a chair nearby, watching.

These boys are all breathing faster. Oxygen is jumping onto those red blood cells, man you bet it's jumping, and rushing back to the heart. Can't wait to get there. Into the left atrium, lub, down to the left ventricle, dub, whoosh up the aorta, red blood cells bouncing off each other in that fast stream, then flying down past the heart, past the stomach, past the intestines, to the internal iliac, starting to slow down some, pudendal artery, dorsal artery, walls getting narrow, harder to move, going slower, blood cells crowding against each other, pushing on the walls, and everything starts to move, all that blood coming in, can't get out, pushing on the muscles, and up they go, up, up, until the cock stands hard, and all the boys have steel club erections. Darrel is running his tongue over Tina's breasts, like he's hungry for a human being.

Desiree has gone to the bathroom and closed the door. Jack has been watching Darrel and Tina, but now he wants his own. He looks around for Desiree, realizes the bag of cocaine is not on the dresser where he left it. "Hey," he says. He stands up and goes to the bathroom door. "Hey," he says again. "Did you fucking take my coke?" He turns the door handle and the door opens.

Desiree is standing there. "Sorry," she says. "I just needed another snort."

"Goddamnit," Jack says. He takes the bag from her hand. "Fucking bag is nearly empty."

"Baby," she says, walking out to the bedroom, "I just took a little extra snort. But I'll make you feel so good you won't

143

even…yeah, you won't even…you…ah, yeah." She closes her eyes and sinks onto the bed.

"Fucking bitch," Jack says. "You owe me." He shoves her short skirt up around her waist and pulls her panties down.

Tina is looking at Desiree on the bed. "I think something's wrong with her," she says, and pushes Darrel away. "I think she's overdosed."

"Hey, she's alright," Darrel says. "What are you doing? She's just passed out. We're just getting going here."

"You can't overdose on cocaine," Jack says.

"What the fuck do you know?" Tina says angrily. She finds her bra on the floor and begins to put it on.

"Hey, what are you doing?" Darrel says.

"She's passed out. That's not alright."

"I'm telling you," Jack says. "You don't overdose on cocaine. I've studied medicine."

Tina picks up her blouse and puts it on. "I'm going to go get help." A minute later she is out the door.

"Well, fuck it," Darrel says. "Fuck this. She blueballed me."

"It's this whore's fault," Jack says, looking down at the half-nude Desiree.

She half opens her eyes, mumbles "Baby," then closes them again.

Young Anthony is still downstairs, and he wants help, too. He stands up from the blackjack table, stares across the room for a moment, lost, wild, all reason and hope out of his brain. He walks across the room, past Julius Caesar, down a flight of stairs to street level, walking for no reason, going nowhere, then stopping. *Lord,* he prays, *help me fix this. Please help me out of this. I'm sorry I took Pop's money. Help me and I'll start seminary in the fall. I swear to it. Please, Lord.* As he prays, he starts to cross himself and feels the gold cross he is wearing underneath his shirt. He holds his hand there, touching the cross, then continues to walk, out of the building, out to the sidewalk. *Please, Lord, please.*

We Give Cash for Gold. Did God put a pawn shop between Caesars and Trump Plaza? Look this way, ye desperate, see this beacon of hope, see this place of refuge, where the drowning find land, where the hanged find knives to cut the rope in time, where those who have lost belief find new faith. "Forty dollars," the old woman says. She turns Anthony's cross around in her hand. "It's a nice piece."

"It cost a lot more than that," Anthony says. "My grandfather gave it to me."

"You want me to pay you for having a grandmother, too? Forty dollars. You want to pawn it?"

This is it, Anthony. At the blackjack table, he leans forward feverishly, his chips like bombs ready to blow him into euphoria or despair. Fatima has learned not to show surprise at people like this, not to say to them, *What are you doing?* She gives him another stack of red chips. His mouth is dry.

Upstairs, Darrel is nervous. "Hey, we got coke in here. What if she brings security?"

"I'll hide the coke," Jack says. "It's not a problem."

"Yeah, nothing's ever a fucking problem for you," Darrel says.

"We can't leave her like this," Francis says. "Maybe she does need a doctor." He pulls Desiree's panties back on her, then stands up. "Maybe we can wake her up."

"Does she look like she's waking up?" Jack says.

"I don't want a girl passed out in my room," Darrel says. "Any trouble with the law could fuck me up getting in the Marine band." He looks at Francis, who is kneeling beside Desiree. "You, too, Florence Nightingale. You want to go in the Army and kill people, you can't be a criminal."

"Alright," Jack says. "Give me a minute." He goes out into the hall, then comes back a minute later.

"There's a chair in the hall just around the corner. Let's put her down there in that chair."

"What if she needs help?" Francis says.

"Jesus Christ!" Jack says. "She's fine. She's fucking passed out from stealing too much coke."

Jack and Darrel pick Desiree up. She's not heavy. Francis hesitates, then opens the door. One minute later Jack and Darrel are back. Easy.

"I've got to have a cigarette," Francis says. He goes in the bathroom.

Ten minutes later, Tina knocks on the door. "They're sending medical help," she says. She hasn't been around the corner to see Desiree slumped in the chair.

"Don't need it," Jack says. "She woke up and said she changed her mind. Said she was going home." Tina stares at him, then looks at the bed, then around the room.

"Where is she?"

"What did I just tell you? I told you, you can't OD on coke. She woke up, she was high, and she said she wanted to go home. You shouldn't have run off like that."

Tina looks around the room again, but there's no Desiree visible here. "Home," she says.

"That's what I'm telling you."

Tina must not have a trusting nature, from that look on her face. Ugly look. "She wouldn't go home," she says. "She hates being at home."

"She's not here," Jack says. "Look around." Tina just looks at Jack, ugly expression, ugly damn expression, turns around and goes out.

"We've got to get out of here," Darrel says. He starts quickly gathering things. "Unless one of you wants to be sitting here when security finds that girl." They grab their bags, and Francis thinks to take Anthony's belongings as well.

When they come out of the elevator below they pass customers in T-shirts and baseball caps, in cheap blazers and nylon pants, men going bald and women with gray hair. What is that noise at the gaming tables? Anthony? The good and noble Anthony is making a speech in praise of Caesars? No, he's

149

pointing at the dealer Fatima, yelling at her. "You cheated me on that last deal! This game is crooked!"

Where do they keep themselves, those guards who suddenly appear when you yell at the staff in a casino? Were you paying attention the last time you did this? They have Anthony by each arm. "No!" he yells, hasty, foolish maybe, twirls around, pulls an arm free, fingers in a fist, smack into a guard. Like triple gravity he plunges to the floor, guards on him.

People watch this wonderful lucky spectacle, Anthony yelling, guards dragging him away. Jack and Darrel hotfoot through the casino area toward the Forum. There's friendship and there's foolhardy volunteering for someone else's problem. Francis hesitates a moment, moves toward Anthony, stands paralyzed with indecision, then turns and hurries after Jack and Darrel, and they cross the bridge under the watchful gaze of multiple Caesars, into the parking garage.

The adrenal glands of these boys are in high gear, secreting adrenaline like a bottle of beer shaken up and the cap

150

popped off. Adrenaline washes through their bodies and moves their feet like their ass is on fire. The adrenaline goes whooping through the blood, smacking into adrenergic receptors, setting off chemical cascades. Woohoo! Speed up the heart beat, send blood rushing more quickly through the body, pour more glucose out, get some energy going, widen up the pupils of the eyes, the better to see the sights as they take their leave of Caesars. The car doors slam, Francis reaches for a cigarette, hands shaking. Yes, he wants to smoke, wants to suck that warm drug down into his lungs, wants to feel calmer, wants…

"Start the fucking car," Jack says.

No one says anything for a long time as they drive, but after they pass the first toll plaza, Jack seems to relax, reaches up to turn on the radio. "Anthony'll be OK," he says. "One night in jail won't hurt him, then he'll call his dad to come get him out. We had an adventure."

"Lucky Tony needs to learn how to behave in a casino," Darrel says.

They drive a few more miles as Francis fills the car up with nervous cigarette smoke. Jack turns around in his seat to address Darrel as well as Francis. "So how much did you guys win at the slots?"

A Sharp Knife for Cutting Limes

I probably wouldn't be in Mexico if there hadn't of been a knife on the counter at Bad Dog Bar last Tuesday. I been going to Bad Dog for two years, since I been working the graveyard shift at Drake Manufacturing. If you ever spent eight hours attaching table tops to the leg frames, you know why that kind of work goes better if you got a couple of beers in you.

One of the evening bartenders at Bad Dog is Hitch. He was working last Tuesday with Sheila, who waits tables. She ain't much of a waitress, to put it gentle. She gets orders wrong every night, even in a place like Bad Dog where most everybody orders the same cheap beer. Sheila's popular, though, with them low-cut blouses. Most of the Bad Dog customers are guys that don't care what they're drinking as long as they're looking down a woman's blouse. That's one of the reasons my brother, Toby, liked Bad Dog right away when he started going there. Plus he didn't have to walk far after work to get there. Then he got me to

153

going. And I gotta say about Sheila and them low-cut blouses, when you look down that valley, you know there's a better world waiting when you get there.

I've got to know a lot of the guys that come in Bad Dog, like Mitt Reagan, a short little guy that keeps a dog cage on the back seat in his car. He walks around like he's six foot six, proud as a prince. I seen where he lives and I seen his girlfriend, and I don't know what he's proud of. Mitt's the kind of guy that'll buy you beers as long as you want to drink, but while he's getting drunk with you, he'll decide to go outside and kick your ass. Another guy that comes in the bar a lot is Carp Shumanski. Carp's so thin he looks weak, like he's sick or something. But he ain't just thin or sick looking, he's crazy, and I ain't just talking "where's my UFO" crazy. I mean the kind of crazy that makes big guys who'd fight a cop try to avoid conversations with Carp. I didn't see it myself, but a couple of people told me he went postal special delivery once on a big Hungarian guy, screaming at the top of his lungs, crying like a girl, grabbing everything his hands touched, every glass, every bottle, even chairs, and flinging them at that Hungarian guy. Then Carp jumped on the guy and tried to bite out his throat. Naturally, the big guy defended himself. They say that's why Carp limps a little bit now.

But most of the guys that come in Bad Dog, they're just regular guys. They work, they hate their job, they drink. You know what I mean, normal working guys. Bad Dog is a place to go before or after work, depending on what your job is like. That's why my brother started going there. A month later, when I get out of jail for something I ain't done this time, Toby, my oldest brother, helped me to get on at Drake Manufacturing. Probably kept me from going back to jail, the mood I was in. I got a younger brother, that useless Ray that still lives with Mama and has him a different career plan once a year. Electrician, computer programmer, day-care worker... But I don't want to talk about Ray.

Toby was in the army and spent time in Kuwait during that first war, shooting rockets across the desert. He liked doing that, and I always liked hearing him talking about how much fun it was shooting them rockets. "Fourth of July every day, man." That was Toby's description of being in Kuwait. When he got out of the army, there wasn't much call to fire rockets in Cincinnati, so Toby got on at Drake. Me and Toby spent some time together at Bad Dog when we was on the same shift, giving eyes to Sheila and arguing over whose turn it was to pay for the beer. Lot of the time, though, Toby paid. He was that kind of brother.

So last Tuesday, Toby comes down to Bad Dog and he sees a guy he don't hardly know, a middle-aged guy named Riley, talking to Sheila. It turns out, Riley has decided he's in love with Sheila, even though Sheila has reached the limit of any potential she ever had. So Sheila's talking to Riley, and Toby's waiting to order a beer, which he could of done at the bar, but he's already sat down and he's waiting on Sheila to come take

156

his order. I wasn't there but I know what all happened because Hitch, the bartender, told me about it.

Toby finally got tired of waiting and he said, "Hey, Sheila, point them things at somebody else for a minute and get me a beer." Sheila turned around and went to the bar, and Hitch said Riley looked kind of pissed. Hitch took to watching Riley, who looked more pissed whenever Sheila took another beer to Toby and when she'd laugh at something Toby said. Later on in the evening, after Toby had drank several beers and was going to take a leak, he went by Riley's table, and Riley said something too low to hear, but Toby just laughed and kept walking. Riley was ordering boilermakers, beer and whiskey, and he'd drank several before he went up to the bar where Sheila was back behind it talking to Hitch. When I talked to Hitch later, he said Riley wanted Sheila to go outside and talk to him, but Hitch said no, she was working. "I ain't talking to you, goddamnit!" Riley said real loud. Hitch ain't too much bothered by loud drunks, or he's working in the wrong bar, so he just told Riley again that Sheila was working and she wasn't going nowhere.

While they was arguing about this, Toby come up to the bar and told Hitch he wanted to pay up and get on. When Toby said that, Riley turned around and looked at him, and Hitch said right then he could see how drunk Riley was.

"You the problem," Riley said to Toby. "You been flirting with Sheila all night."

Toby laughed at Riley and said, "I ain't in competition with you, old man." Hitch said it was surprising somebody as drunk as Riley could move so fast, because he grabbed a knife off the bar and swung it at Toby. Hitch started yelling and Sheila started screaming when blood sprayed all over the bar. Riley had cut a vein in Toby's neck, and by the time the ambulance and police got there, Toby was dead and Riley had run out the door.

Riley's picture was in the paper the next day, and I found out there was people at the factory didn't like Riley too much. He was a bad-tempered guy who knew how to piss people off. One of them told me Riley was always talking about this place in Luna Perdida, Mexico, said he was gonna go there someday. I seen him a few days ago, but right now I'm sitting here in the Alocate Bar in Luna Perdida, thinking about how I used to go fishing with Toby, thinking about how Mama kind of wilted after Toby died.

Here in the bar they got Christmas lights all over like they don't know it's April. And they got some band on the loudspeakers, some German group, playing over and over real loud like they was God almighty. I don't mind loud music, but I kind of like to know what they're saying. I'm tired of the music, but I ain't leaving the bar yet. I'm ordering me another margarita. They do a good margarita here, with Mexican limes, better than the kind we got back home. The bartender is cutting the limes right on the bar. So I'm gonna order me another margarita, and then I'm gonna go walk down a particular alley where Riley goes every evening. When he comes along I'm gonna say, "Hey, remember my brother, Toby?" And then I'm gonna pull out that knife that's laying right there on the bar and

shove it in his heart.

Snow Fool

"Beer beer beer!"

The first time I saw Snow Fool I was five years old, sitting on my grandmother's front porch. The first time, anyway, that I remember seeing him. I must have seen him before, but this time stuck into my memory. Maybe because he was standing in the snow, so that I remembered it on account of his nickname.

I was sitting there with my grandmother, who had her hair tied in a long braid in the back, a braid her sister did for her on Sunday mornings after Granny had washed her hair on Saturday night. A big bag of walnuts was on the porch between us, and we were cracking and shelling. Mostly I was smashing the nuts with a hammer and eating what could be saved from the wreckage. So there we sat, Granny in a cane chair my grandfather had woven, and down the road came Snow Fool.

Snow Fool had a name, a Christian name, just like all the other Christians in the mountains where we lived. His name was Jace, which was short for Jorace, but it might as well have been

Alexander the Great, because nobody called him either one. I don't even know how I found out his name; all I ever heard him called was Snow Fool, or mostly just Fool in the summer.

So yonder came Snow Fool, kicking up clouds of the dry powdery snow, and just like he'd figured out what would most annoy Granny, he was yelling "Beer!" every couple of kicks. Granny tried to ignore him, being a Christian, but being a Christian, she couldn't. "Beer! Beer! Beer!" he shouted, coming on past the house.

As I recall, he stopped, facing the porch, and pulled off his red-and-blue sock cap, which left his hair sticking out like he'd just had electroshock.

"Hey, Miz Stack. Good afternoon. You wouldn't have no bottles of beer there in your house would you? And you, too, little Toby."

Little Toby was me, and I wondered how this stranger knew who I was. He must have remembered seeing me before I remembered seeing him.

"We don't keep beer in this house, Snow. I'm surprised you wouldn't know that."

"I ain't never looked in your refrigerator."

"Well, there's no beer, there never has been. There won't be none while I live."

"Sorry I bothered you, Miz Stack. I'll go on down to the preacher's. I have had occasion to look into his refrigerator. I reckon he'll have some. Beer! Beer!" And off he went in a cloud of snow up to his knees. By the way, Granny was the only one called Snow Fool just Snow, on account, she said, that it says in the Bible not to call anybody a fool. Even if they are one, she'd add.

As he walked off, I went back to cracking nuts and thought no more about him, no longer interested. Granny used to say that my "cattish qualification", my curiosity, was less than what a normal child would have, but I didn't care. Even at that young age, I was the practical person I stayed later in life. I remember Snow Fool now and then, on through the years. I believe he was about eighteen the first time I saw him. He lived with his mother, who was a seamstress in town. They had come to our town, that is to say, the closest town to us, which we called ours, from somewhere in Tage County, the next one over. Snow Fool's daddy was long gone. Years later my uncle told me he remembered Snow Fool's daddy, who, he said, "just lived for the sight of a whore, didn't matter none what color she was". According to my uncle, Snow Fool's daddy had run off to look for "whorehopper heaven". My uncle was a fool himself. He just hid it better.

Another time I remember Snow Fool was when he was just Fool, in the summer, that is. I think I was around ten then, and I was going fishing with my neighbor Jackie, who was my age, and his sister Ann, who was a few years older. The three of us had simple fishing poles, the kind lots of kids carry, that they make themselves. We also had a tin can of worms that Ann had dug up in their back yard.

"Thar comes Fool," said Jackie. We were walking down the paved road where you turned off to the creek. "Damn."

"Can't talk like that, Jackie," Ann said.

"Paw says damn."

"Don't care if Paw does say damn. *You* can't say damn."

"Reckon I damn well can."

"I'll tell Gram, and we'll see who says damn."

While they were busy damning at each other, we met Fool. He was wearing a long-sleeve white shirt and a tie, pretty poorly tied. "Where yall going?" Fool asked.

"We going fishing, Fool," Ann answered.

"What with?"

"Night crawlers."

"Night crawlers. Lemme see." He took the can from Jackie and pulled out one long reddish-black worm, holding it between two fingers. It twisted and curled up over his fingers.

"You ever eat a night crawler, Jackie?"

"No. Ain't gonna, neither."

165

"I believe," said Fool, "you're operating under what the preacher called *pre*judice. You have *pre*judiced against this worm. Cause they mighty tasty." With that he held the thin squirming worm up over his mouth, his head tilted back and his mouth wide open.

"Oh, damn!" Ann yelled. I felt sick and looked down at the ground. Jackie was making a disgusted noise, and when I looked up Ann had her eyes squeezed tight. Fool had his hands down by his side and was half smiling, sucking his teeth.

"You made my stomach hurt," I said.

"It'll feel better if you'll eat one of these." Fool held the can out to me.

I looked away and made a little gagging noise.

"Oh, hell!" Fool spat with disgust. "Yall can't take no joke. I didn't eat that worm." He held it up, still squirming, and dropped it back in the can. "I don't eat worms." He handed the can back to Jackie. "Unless they cooked."

My mouth was all bitter tasting, and *I* sure didn't see no damn joke.

Sometime along in the fall, when folks started thinking about winter, Fool changed into Snow Fool. He got to be called Snow Fool because he didn't seem to mind the cold, but would stay out in the snow, sometimes just sit there, singing or talking to himself or whoever passed by. He could stay out in the snow all day long, wandering around in the mountains, and never get cold. Not that anybody knew, anyway.

Snow Fool wasn't important to anybody, not really. He was a curiosity around the area, but nobody ever thought about him when he wasn't around. The preacher from the Baptist church, where my family went and I was forced to go twice on Sundays, felt sorry for Snow Fool and would have him to dinner a lot, but the preacher never did get him into church. It probably didn't matter, though, 'cause I reckoned he must have preached Snow Fool near to death while he ate. I didn't think Snow Fool minded a bit. I believed he just sat there with a mouth jammed

167

full of cornbread, stretching out his hand for a pork chop, while the preacher told him about the evils of Jezebel. At that time, as a matter of fact, Snow Fool was probably pleased to hear about Jezebel. No matter how much folks preached at him and tried to convert him, he stayed a sinner. At least by the reckoning of kids who I knew, he was a sinner, and they had given a good deal of thought to the subject, just where that line was, and just what you *could* do, as well as what you could do for fun and still be able to repent later.

Snow Fool was not at that time a Christian by the definition I knew. He drank any time he could, the sin in that being that he didn't hide the fact, but was open about it. After we were young men, Jackie told me that Snow Fool "woulda been a whorehopper like his daddy, but he didn't know how". Snow Fool did like women, though, and when he thought he was "with the boys" he would grin and ask us if we had done this or done that. We used to discuss whether Snow Fool had really done those things and whether he even knew what they were. He was the only middle-aged man we knew (him being at the time just past thirty) who'd talk to us like he did. "Did you get it wet last Saturday?" But we thought it was pretty funny to have Snow Fool come leering up saying such things. Most of us figured that Snow Fool had never done it, because what woman in her right mind would want to get in bed with him? Jackie also told me that Gus Grady had caught Snow Fool jerking off in his barn. Jackie was simply an encyclopedia of sin.

As I got older and began to work more seriously, my interest in Snow Fool decreased because he didn't have anything to do with how I lived. I figured we're just here to work hard, and what choice do you have? For people around me, religion was like the water they lived in, and if that's what they wanted, they could have it, but that stuff didn't mean anything to me. When I was twenty-five, I married Jackie's sister Ann. I guessed she was glad to marry me, as she was getting pretty well up there for anyone to be courting her. Besides which, we'd been going to bed together for two years, and both of us sort of felt, though I don't recall either one ever mentioning it, that that kind of gave us a reason to get married. She didn't get pregnant then, though, because she used to jump up and down after we were done. It was a trick she had learned from an older cousin over in Tage County. But anyhow, I didn't marry her from obligation, but because I wanted to. If I hadn't of, I wouldn't of. After we were married, Ann quit jumping up and down, and we had a daughter. And around that time I've got stretches of years in my memory when I can't remember anything in particular about Snow Fool.

But he was always around. We buried my blind old Granny, and later in the afternoon, after the funeral, I was walking in the woods thinking about this death business, why we have to do that, when I ran into Snow Fool. It was January, and I had on a heavy coat, a fur hat, and mittens. He had a lot lighter coat than mine, a grey cap on top of his head, not covering his ears, and no gloves or mittens.

I came on him real sudden. He was sitting on a log that was still covered with snow. "Toby," he said.

I jumped, because the woods were so quiet, and I didn't know he was there. I saw him and felt a little irritated, but I wasn't sure why. Why didn't he feel the cold?

"It's me."

"Snow Fool."

"Sitting in the snow." He grinned. Anyone else I'd have wondered if they weren't cold, but I knew he wasn't. Or if he was, he didn't know it.

"Sorry about your Granny," he said.

"How'd you know?"

"Preacher told me"

"Oh. Yeah."

"I'll have a service for her this evening."

"Do what?" It was the usual nonsense, but I said, "I didn't think you believed in church."

"Depends on whose church it is. If it's my church, I don't mind none." He picked up a handful of snow and began to eat.

"Preacher finally get you into church?"

He stopped munching for a second. "Him? Naw." Then he reached for more snow. I wondered what he meant by "my church", but I didn't care enough to ask any more about it.

The next year Snow Fool started doing something he'd never done before. He came by our house Christmas Eve, in the afternoon, carrying a dirty cloth bag, asking us for old biscuits or cornbread. Nobody knew how Snow Fool lived, how he got by. His mother had died several years before and was buried in the cemetery of the Methodist church, which she had attended sometimes. Snow Fool wouldn't go near the Methodist church, even before his mother was buried there. But how he lived and ate after she died, nobody thought enough about him to really wonder a lot about it. Or maybe Preacher thought about it, I don't know. When Snow Fool started coming by asking for bread, it seemed so natural that he was begging that we just wondered why he hadn't done it before.

We invited him in for a meal, offered him a lot more than dry bread, but he surprised me and said if we had any old biscuits he'd be proud, but he didn't need anything else. So we gave him some leftover bread, and he went on his way through the snow, singing "O Little Town of Bethlehem".

From then on, every year Snow Fool came by on Christmas Eve asking for old bread. We always invited him for something more, but he never took anything more than the bread. We figured after a while that he didn't take the bread from hunger, because he never asked for food other than that. It was our daughter, Jeanie, who decided what he wanted the bread for.

"He's feeding the birds." she said, and it seemed reasonable to me. Every year we had bread ready on Christmas Eve for Snow Fool to collect, and he always came by.

One year I was out back chopping wood when Snow Fool came along. He went to the side door, got his bread, and, after stomping a minute on the little porch, went on. I wasn't chopping when he came by but had stopped to rest after fighting a hard knot that I wasn't going to cut through, so I heard his voice saying, "Yall got any old biscuits or cornbread you planning to throw out?" Of course he must have known we did, or he should have known, but he always asked. When I heard him leaving, I suddenly wondered where he was going, just where he took this bread every year. I had always figured he just went and threw it in a field somewhere. That was about all I thought of it, but this year while I was resting, I watched him come out the back door, where the light was slightly glowing around his head from the sun setting in that direction. I don't know why, but I laid the axe on the stump and watched him as he headed off down the road. This time, surprised at myself, I went after him.

I went off into the woods and followed him from there, keeping way back and waiting while he stopped at other houses. Finally he went into the woods himself, and then it was hard for me to keep him in sight without letting him know I was following him. A lot of the time I just followed his tracks and didn't worry that my own tracks would give away that I'd been there. Finally I creeped up over a hill and could hear him talking down below. Lying low, cold, with my face in the snow, I peered over the hill. I saw a clearing, and in the middle of it, an evergreen tree. Snow Fool was standing at the tree using pieces of string to tie the bread on the branches, while he was talking to himself. In a few minutes he had bread hung all over the evergreen like it was a Christmas tree, and he thought the same thing because he was saying, "Here you go, birds, I fixed this here tree for you. Go ahead, it's yours. Nice Christmas tree for the birds."

Then, when he had the tree covered with bread, he went over to the side and sat down in the snow, leaning up against the trunk of a tall sweetgum tree.

I waited a bit to see what he would do, and all the while I was freezing. When I had decided that the crazy damn Snow Fool was just going to sit there and watch the birds eat, he started talking again. A few birds were flying down, pecking at the tree, landing near it.

"Enjoy the Christmas tree, birds. I'm gonna tell yall birds a story while yall are eating and don't notice. There was this baby born somewhere, I can't remember, but he was Jesus. Yall know who Jesus is? I'm gonna tell you. He is the Lord, Lord God. And he was born with these smart men and angels, and he said, 'For God so loved the world he sent me.' Now that's true, it's written down. Now birds, yall listen. If you eat his body, you go to heaven. It ain't nasty, like it sounds, and this cornbread is Jesus's body. I don't know how it is, but it is. And yall gonna go to heaven, too, long as you eat. I guess they's birds in heaven like here." Snow Fool was preaching to the birds.

I had imagined at one time, apparently wrong, that Snow Fool shoved his mouth full of cornbread without paying attention to the preacher. Now the birds did the same for him. While I was watching him, feeling chilled and ready to head home, I looked at the evergreen tree with the bread hanging on it, a few birds already coming in to sit on branches and pick at the bread, and with the last sunlight coming through the trees. It reminded me of a real Christmas tree, of being a kid coming into the room where the tree was. I loved Christmas when I was young. I still do, but for different reasons, and here it suddenly looked like there was a Christmas tree standing in the middle of the woods. I noticed the way the reddish light was on it, then I saw the shadows of other trees like long black lines. All of it struck me like something new, looking at the woods a way I had never seen before, like you could create Christmas just with what was in nature. I lay there for a few more minutes, breathing in the cold air, wanting that scene to last, but seeing the light fade off.

Stiff and shivering, I slid real quiet back down the hill until I could stand up, then I hurried to the main road and home. I caught a cold for Christmas Day.

So Snow Fool preached to the birds, and he was saving their souls with old biscuits. I never followed him again, but I did for years after that go out the day after Christmas to see if he had tied the bread to the tree. and I always found bits of bread and string hanging from it. If there was snow that year, there would be hundreds of tiny bird tracks around the tree.

Like this it went on, a few more years. Snow Fool stayed Snow Fool, and I didn't tell anybody but Ann that he preached to birds. In the summer he was a Fool. and in the winter he was a Snow Fool. But every Christmas Eve there he was, dragging a dirty bag to collect bread, and the day after Christmas, or whenever I got to it, I could find that tree with fresh string hanging off it.

On my forty-second birthday, in July, Jackie came by the store where I worked and asked me if I'd heard. They had found Snow Fool lying beside the road. Doctor said he must have had a heart attack. So it happened that Snow Fool didn't get buried in his forest church. but in the cemetery of the Baptist church. The preacher, who was a pretty old man then, wanted it. He wasn't really the preacher anymore—they had a younger man—but he still went there, and he said he knew Snow Fool had been a Baptist in his heart, so they allowed him to be buried there.

That year, when Christmas Eve came, I started putting some biscuits on a plate without thinking about it, then remembered about Snow Fool dying. The biscuits lay on the plate all afternoon. Late in the day, when the sun was red, I saw them, went and got my coat on, and got some string. I put the bread in a paper bag and went quiet out the side door. It was getting pretty dark in the woods, but I found the clearing where Snow Fool had his tree. Pretty quick I tied the bread on the strings and the strings on the tree. For a few minutes I stood off to one side to see if the birds would come, but it was late for them to be out, so I went back home.

The next year, though, I went out earlier, and this time I saw the birds come and eat. Every year after that I put bread on Snow Fool's tree for the birds. Or for Snow Fool. I don't know. And every year, I remembered the time I watched him preaching to the birds, when I lay there and watched the light coming through the trees.

The Only Person in the World

It's not a crime to stutter, but you can be convicted for it. Or if you're a fourteen-year-old girl in high school, stuttering might actually *be* a crime, a subcrime of the law against being different. Claudia stuttered most of the time if people were around, but especially in a group, when it was worst. To try to stop the stuttering she would squeeze her left hand into a hard fist, the fingernails cutting into her palm, and then speak slowly, breathing deeply. It rarely worked. Speaking slowly only meant stuttering slowly, which she was sure created a false impression of her intellectual ability.

"Sucrose is a di- di- disacch- saccharide," she said in biology class. The teacher always called on Claudia, not to torture her, which of course it always did, but because Claudia was the only person other than the teacher who always knew the answer. Claudia never volunteered to answer, but she was good in biology. After her moment of torture, she would escape by looking down at her notebook, where she had filled the margins with sketches of things that were difficult to draw: saxophones, roses, seagulls. Because they were difficult, she drew them over and over, trying to get them right.

Silently, in her head, she said *disaccharide,* pronouncing it perfectly. *Disaccharide, disaccharide.*

She did the drawings in other classes, however, because she loved biology and always paid attention. For her, science, and biology in particular, was the whole world. She always wore a charm, even when bathing, in the shape of a DNA molecule, a gift from her aunt one Christmas. Everything around her she saw as a complex web of biological connections, with the movement of carbon atoms from sugar to starch, amino acids forming proteins, water moving through the bodies of plants and animals, hearts beating, seeds germinating to make the world green, plants and animals serving as food, and all of them going back to the earth to duplicate the cycle. Of course there were less interesting things that didn't take part in this biology web—cars, stores, dishes, clothes. All the important things, however, were definitely in the ancient cycle of life that was still new every day—the fields of tomatoes and peppers, corn that rustled taller every day across the road, the flocks of Canada geese that passed honking overhead to settle on the pond where frogs lived, the patch of trees behind the house, where dogwoods bloomed in spring and oaks in the fall went magical with red and yellow, and even clouds, which brought rain to water the plants. Claudia loved the beautiful farmland where she lived, loved Salem County and its meadows and forests and creeks and fields of vegetables, fruits, and grains.

The most important things in all the great world of biology were Claudia's two Angora goats, Rosie and Frank, named for Rosalind Franklin, the woman who'd helped discover DNA. Claudia also loved her parents, who ran the farm, but although Claudia would never have said so, and didn't quite realize it, she felt more affection for the goats. Since she had no true friends otherwise, in her most intimate, personal world there lived Claudia, Rosie, and Frank.

Along with her belief in the ability of science to explain the mechanisms of the world, Claudia also believed that clouds hold secrets about the future. When she was nine she'd had a real friend, Gillian, who had told her about how the stars affect people. Gillian said the stars make some people happy and some people mad all the time, and if you could read the stars, you'd know what your future would be. Claudia and Gillian once sat in lawn chairs in Gillian's back yard looking up at the stars, talking about how it could be possible for stars to affect people, and they decided that stars must be sending rays to Earth. Afterward, they sat there holding out their tongues, purple from eating popsicles, trying to catch star rays on the tips. Only a couple of years later, after Gillian's family moved to Arizona, Claudia realized that the rays from the stars must come down in the daytime as well, even though you couldn't see the stars. This idea came to her on a day when the clouds were thick across the sky and in fast motion, gray-and-white masses, swirling and changing, a day when she was looking for ticks on one of the dogs. As she knelt beside the dog, her hands parting his thick fur, she looked up at the sky and it came to her. Star rays coming to Earth would have to pass through the clouds, so the shapes of the clouds could be affected by the stars. She had paused in surprise, thinking about this idea. Maybe if you understood the shapes of the clouds you could see what the future would be. She found a tick, grimaced, and plucked it off.

"The stars say you die," she said.

Perhaps the stars affect us more on cloudy days. It seemed to Claudia that she felt a little differently on days when the sky was covered with clouds. This had been a summer of clouds, so many colors and shapes that she could not grow tired of watching them.

One day in July she stopped on her way out to the barn to look up at the celestial panorama. Off in the direction of Woodstown, the horizon was covered with orange clouds, some bright orange, with a few white ones along the edges, and all in circular shapes. Maybe the circular shapes meant that things would go around and come back. There were days when the vault of the sky was nothing but empty blue, but sometimes an entire drama was happening up there, if only you knew how to read it. She continued on to the barn and said, "Rosie, Frank, anybody hungry?"

The goats came to the edge of their pens and bleated at her. Because they were male and female and she didn't want to breed them, they were penned separately. Rosie was more than two years old and Frank just over one year. "Hey, guys, hey, guys," Claudia said, leaning over the edge of the pens to scratch each goat on the head. "How you doing, huh?" She checked their water, then gave each of them a fresh bundle of hay and a pan of yellow corn. The Salem County Fair was in August, over a month away, and Rosie was going to win the Angora goat contest. Not to take anything away from Frank, but Rosie had a perfect shape, and her fleece was long and soft and had a good wave to it. Claudia had watched the contest for the last two years, and she knew that this year the first-place ribbon was just waiting to go to Rosie. After feeding the goats, Claudia checked them over. She paid close attention to her goats, and in addition to inspecting them for any problems, she enjoyed petting them, feeling the shape of their muscles and running her hands through the long, fine mohair fleece. Sometimes when she felt unhappy or lonely, she would come to the pens to check on the goats, then spend a while sitting and petting them. At the same time she would talk, telling them things she didn't tell anyone else.

"It's my time of the month," she said as she stroked Frank. "I still can't tell when it's coming and my panties were bloody this morning. It's kind of scary." Claudia considered Frank and Rosie friends, and this made great sense to her, since she knew that animals have souls and she would see them again in heaven after they died.

Before leaving the pens, she took out the notebook she kept in a wooden box on the wall and made notes on what she had just done and on the general condition of the goats. She was meticulous in record keeping, not only because she would need some of that information for the contest, but because she cared about Rosie and Frank and wanted to carefully monitor how they were doing, when they had been treated for parasites, how much they ate, and so on. In her note taking, she also tried to spell everything correctly, believing that good scientists would spell properly.

After she had recorded what she just fed them, she began to sketch a rose in the margin, but then heard a noise on the other side of the barn. Her father was on the other side with Sergio and Luis, two of the Mexican men he hired in the summer. The three of them were beginning to load a truck with plastic crates, which hired workers would fill up tomorrow with bright ripe tomatoes.

"Hey, D- Dad," Claudia said. "Is Mom in the h- h- house?"

"Yeah, I think so," he said, then turned to one of the men working with him. "Sergio, no quiero la caja grande."

"OK," Sergio said.

Claudia ran back to the house, but detoured by the flowerbed to pick several red and pink zinnias. She came in through the kitchen door and found her mother at the counter rolling out dough.

"Z- zinnias, Mom," Claudia said. "I n- need a vase."

"Look on the shelves behind the door," her mother said.

"Oh," Claudia said. "Are y- y- you making p- pies?"

"Two peach pies. One for us and one for Molly."

Claudia's family used to go with Molly and Jack to the Cowtown Rodeo in the summer, near the fairground, to watch the riding and roping, but last spring Jack had died from pancreatic cancer. Since then Claudia's family tried to help Molly out, especially because she had two children.

Claudia opened the closet and took a vase from one of the shelves built onto the back of the door. She was humming unaware as she chose the vase, and as she took it her mind moved from Molly's house to travel down the road, to a white house with a long driveway lined with roses. A sign at the end of

189

the driveway, by the road, said "Eternal Hope Farm". As Claudia filled the vase with water and put in the zinnias, she saw the sign in her mind. The Vail family, who attended the same church as Claudia's family, ran the farm. The family was neither here nor there to Claudia, with the clear exception of Grady Vail. He was Claudia's age, and just before school ended in the spring, she had been surprised to find herself dreaming about this boy who she had scarcely paid attention to before. He had straight brown hair, long enough that it came down onto his neck, and it seemed to her that he smiled a lot. She could barely take her eyes away from him and was sometimes horrified to think he might realize she was smitten. She was glad he went to her church, so she could still see him during the summer, but she would never have dreamed of actually going up to talk to him.

Thinking entirely of Grady now, she carried the vase out to the hallway and put it on the table where her mother often had vases of flowers. Thoughts of Grady made her feel... made her feel... she didn't know how, a sort of stirred-up feeling, happy and anxious at the same time. One way she had found to calm herself down was to read poems of Emily Dickinson. She went up to her room, sat on her bed, and opened the book.

> It's all I have to bring today—
> This, and my heart beside—
> This, and my heart, and all the fields—
> And all the meadows wide—
> Be sure you count—should I forget
> Some one the sum could tell—
> This, and my heart, and all the Bees
> Which in the Clover dwell.

She read through the poem a second time, and already the emotional swirl within her began to calm. For another half hour she continued to read. When she put the book down, she sat at her dresser and looked at herself in the mirror, then lifted her hair up off her neck, holding it to the left, then the right, then pulling it back. She wondered if she should get it cut somehow.

The next Sunday, the teacher asked which of the young people in Claudia's Sunday-school class had read the Bible lesson, which they all claimed to have done. Grady was in the class as well, always sitting with his friends Justin and Jarad.

"Why was God angry at David?" the teacher asked.

"Because he wanted to get married," a girl said, and some of the kids laughed.

"No, not because he wanted to get married," the teacher said. "Do you know, Claudia?"

No no no! Why did he have to ask her? She glanced up, and Grady was looking at her. Why did the teacher ask her a question about David's girlfriend? Claudia felt herself turning red. "Be- be- because he w- w- was, because D- D- David w- was—" She paused to slow down, gripped her hand into a fist, then stopped altogether, looking at the floor and wondering if there was a way to suffer more than this. Why did the stupid Sunday-school teacher have to embarrass her?

Driving home from church, she wished she could forget the great lake of humiliation she had just drowned in. Yet it was a beautiful sunny summer day, with a cloudless blue sky. As they drove, she looked out at green fields that rolled just slightly, with stands of trees on the far edge framing the crops. Those

192

fields were replaced by corn, which lined the road so that nothing could be seen but the wall of leafy stalks, then suddenly there was a farmhouse yard with flowers. She felt calmer by the time they arrived home.

Later that week Claudia was sitting at the dining table wearing her Philadelphia Phillies T-shirt, eating her usual breakfast of Cheerios with chocolate milk, when her mother came in with a basket of clean towels and asked her to fold them. Before leaving the room, her mother said, "Oh, I just heard something that I thought would be interesting to you. One of the boys in your Sunday-school class is going to enter the Angora goat contest at the fair. Molly said Grady Vail raises Angora goats, too."

Her mother then left the room, not noticing how long Claudia's spoon hung motionless in the air. Her mother did notice an hour later that Claudia had not folded the towels and had gone back to bed, lying there with her hands over her eyes. "Are you sick?" her mother asked.

"I d- don't feel good."

"Is it another migraine?"

"Yes," Claudia said, in order to be allowed to lie there, then felt worse with guilt for lying. In a moment her mother came back and laid a cold cloth across Claudia's eyes and forehead.

"I'll check on you again in a little while," she said. Claudia rolled over and put her arms around the large brown stuffed dog, Brownie, that she had slept with since she was two years old. She pushed her face into Brownie's worn side, hiding her face from the world.

"No," she whispered, "no."

Grady was in the contest. The contest was one of the best things she had, a chance for people to look at her and see her as good at something, as a capable person who knew what she was doing. She wouldn't have to speak, just watch her perfect goat win. But when she thought about Grady, her image of him made her feel warm, almost happy. How could she win the contest against someone who she felt that way about? She imagined winning and looking over to see him as the loser, and already the imagined pleasure of winning was less.

She sighed heavily and pulled the cloth off her eyes, then looked out the window. Off on the horizon the sky was dark with clouds in large rolling shapes. Since they were dark, did that mean the future would be bad? The present was certainly bad.

It rained that afternoon, so that Claudia's father was in the house early, complaining about needing to harvest peppers. Hunger finally drove Claudia up from bed. She ate a late lunch of tomato sandwiches, then sat on the side porch watching the rain blur the patch of woods behind the house.

The next day she went out to the goat pens with a heavy heart, knowing she was going to misuse her friends. In Heaven, where they would be able to talk, they would remind her of this. "Hey, guys," she said without enthusiasm as she approached the pens. As usual they came to the edge of the pens and bleated at her. "How you doing, guys?" she said, feeling dejected but trying to show some brightness. "You hungry?"

After she had fed them, she knelt down by Rosie and petted the goat for a while, then said, "I'm sorry, Rosie. I'm going to put Frank in the contest. I know you're a winner, I know you'd beat all the other goats, but that's why I have to go with Frank. There's a boy who's going to have his goat in the contest, and I can't win against him. I don't know if you can understand that. I guess another goat doesn't make you feel like Grady makes me feel. All you have to think about is eating and being a goat. I'm really sorry, Rosie, but I can't help it." She stopped and sighed, and rubbed Rosie on the head. "I can't help it. You could still have a chance next year." Rosie leaned over and took another mouthful of hay.

That Sunday at church Claudia watched Grady from a distance as usual, feeling her heart fill up from being near him. She had been anxious about going back to church after stuttering herself into speechlessness, but she couldn't tell her parents she didn't want to go, and she also wanted to see Grady. As always he sat with his friends and didn't even seem to notice that she existed. That was probably best. So she sat with a heart that yearned, hardly even knowing why it yearned. After the preaching service, before people dispersed, she carefully placed herself on the porch of the church, then moved around near the parking lot, very casually, very naturally, so as to keep an eye on him.

For nearly two weeks after she'd learned that Grady had a goat in the contest at the county fair, she had been preparing her second goat, Frank, instead of Rosie. These days she checked him a little more diligently than before, carefully undid the slightest tangle in his fleece, and checked his feed to make sure it was exactly right. "You'll do fine, Frank," she said. "Lots of goats would like to place. You don't have to be first." She also wondered frequently what Grady's goat was like. She didn't know how to find out, so she imagined a beautiful goat with silky fleece, and she pictured Grady feeding and petting it. She wished for him to have the most beautiful goat at the fair, a strange feeling that seemed to combine both goodness and badness, but she wanted Grady to win.

The second Sunday after she switched from Rosie to Frank, she was again slipping about at church with careful casualness to keep sight of Grady. This time she found herself behind a bush and couldn't see him but could hear his voice. He, Justin, and Jarad were talking to two girls from school.

"We're going to the shore next week," Jarad said.

"Where are you going?" one of the girls asked.

"We rent a house for a week at Ocean City."

"Oh, I love Ocean City," the girl said.

"You l- l- love Ocean City?" a voice said. Claudia froze. "What d- d- d- you d- d- do there?" The other kids laughed. "D-do you s- swim?" It was Grady talking.

"No," the girl said. "I l- l- lie on the b- b- beach."

They all laughed again, and Grady added, "I'd s- swim."

Her knees shaking, her face aching from the effort not to cry, Claudia walked quickly across the lawn to the parking lot, found their car, and got in. By the time her parents checked the car to see if she was there, she was lying across the back seat sobbing.

"Claudia!" her mother said with alarm. "What's wrong?"

"N- n- no," Claudia said and continued to cry with her face covered. She was hoping that she might die before they reached the house, but then they pulled into the driveway. Ignoring her parents, she jumped out of the car and ran toward the woods.

"Claudia!" her mother yelled.

"She'll come back when she's ready," her father said.

For a long time she lay on the ground in the woods crying. If she could just become part of the earth, turn into the soil, be part of the biological world where there wasn't any speaking. In the biological world things lived and died because it was the natural way, not because they were miserable and wanted to die.

After an hour, feeling drained, she came out of the woods and walked toward the barn. Her good clothes were covered with dirt and leaves, and several twigs clung to her hair. She glanced up at the sky where she saw blue emptiness, nothing more. Without saying anything she went to the goat pens and climbed in with Rosie. She knelt, put her arms around the goat's neck, and said, "You'll be happy when you win, girl. You'll be happy, won't you?" Claudia put her face on Rosie's neck, then stood up. "Let's get you ready."

Dragon Lessons

When your mom wakes you up really early in the summer, it should be for something good, like going to New Jersey to the shore. That's a good day, because you can play on the beach, jump at the waves, walk on the boardwalk and look at all the funny people, and eat very good things like fudge and pizza. That's what happened for Terrell, who was already eight years old and knew a lot of stuff, and his sister Shalitha, who was six and liked to know what Terrell knew. Terrell and Shalitha had fun playing together, and they were very happy when Mom and Dad said they would go to the shore on Friday.

There was just one problem. From Philadelphia to the shore was a really really long way and it took forever and ever and you'd get very bored. You could play with your brother or sister in the backseat, but eventually your Mom would tell you to stop making so much noise, and then it would get boring again. You could still whisper together so your mom wouldn't know what you were talking about. That was OK. When Terrell and

Shalitha had been riding in the car forever and ever, and Dad had told them twice to quit asking because they would be there soon, they finally saw some water. It wasn't the ocean, but at least it was water.

Then Terrell saw something fly by and go behind some trees.

"A blue heron," Mom said.

Terrell didn't know what it was she saw, but he had seen something fly behind the trees, and it looked like it might be big and mean. Maybe it was bigger than it looked. Maybe it had scales—he didn't see it too good. Maybe it was breathing fire just a little bit. "I saw a dragon," he said.

"What's a dragon?" Shalitha asked.

"It's a big lizard monster," Terrell said.

"Terrell!" Mom said. "Don't tell her things like that. You're going to give her bad dreams."

Shalitha looked over at her brother and made a face with a round O mouth.

"I just told her—" Terrell started. Mom turned around in her seat and looked at him. "OK," he said.

In a little while they drove around a circle and up on a bridge, and then they really could see water, for real this time, with boats in it.

"There's Ocean City up ahead," Dad said. And they saw a big Ferris wheel over there, bigger than a house. Shalitha liked to see Ferris wheels, even if there was no way she would get on one. This time, though, she was looking at Terrell instead.

When they came off the bridge, she leaned over and whispered, "What's a dragon?"

He whispered back, "They fly around and breathe fire."

"Fire?" she whispered, and looked astonished. Terrell glanced toward the front seat and nodded yes.

After Dad parked the car, they walked up a big wooden sidewalk that went up off the ground. When they got up to the top there were a lot of people walking around.

"Here's the boardwalk," Dad said. "We'll do things up here until lunchtime, and then we'll go down to the beach after lunch."

"What's a boardwalk," Shalitha asked.

Terrell laughed. "It's made out of boards," he said. "And we're walking on it."

"Oh," Shalitha said. "I want to walk on it too."

The boardwalk was really *huge*, as big as a street, with lots of people. On one side it had stores and even a movie theater. Before they had walked very far, before they had even barely got started and they weren't even thinking of doing anything wrong, Mom said, "Wait. Let me tell you a couple of rules. You can both have one thing to eat or drink this morning, we'll have lunch later, and you can have one thing to eat or drink in the afternoon. And you can each have a souvenir that doesn't cost over ten dollars."

"Why do we always have rules everywhere we go?" Terrell asked.

"Because we're with children," Mom said. Sometimes she would say things like that that didn't make any sense.

There were a hundred people on the boardwalk, maybe even a thousand. There were lots of kids, and some of them had ice cream cones or candy or hotdogs. There were older kids in groups, who got to walk around by themselves, and lots of adults walking around too. Everybody had on bathing suits or shorts, and it was hot. It was hot as dragon fire. Some people were riding bicycles, but the most very cool thing was bicycles connected together with seats on top of the bicycles, like benches, and a little roof. A bunch of people could ride together in those.

"Mom," Terrell said, "let's ride those bikes."

"Yeah, yeah! Mom! Mom!" Shalitha said. "Let's ride in those cars."

"Let's look in some of the shops," Mom said. She must not have heard what they said.

"Maybe we'll ride later," Dad said.

They went in a store, and Dad started trying on hats and looking funny.

"How's this one?" he said. He looked goofy, because it was a big pink hat with flowers on it. Shalitha started laughing, so Dad looked at Terrell and said, "What do you think? Your sister thinks it looks good on me."

Terrell laughed too and said, "Yeah, you look like Grammy." Shalitha laughed even more to think about Dad looking like Grammy. Finally Dad bought a straw hat, because Mom said he needed to keep the sun off his head.

"The sun makes me dopey," Dad said, and made a silly face.

When they left the hat store, Dad and Mom walked ahead, and Shalitha asked Terrell, "What do dragons look like?"

"They're big," Terrell said. "They're big and huge."

"As big as Dad?"

"Way bigger than Dad."

"As big as a car?"

"Bigger than a truck."

Shalitha tried to imagine this. "How can it be bigger than a truck?"

"An elephant's bigger than a truck."

"Oh, yeah. Is a dragon bigger than an elephant?"

"Even bigger than an elephant." Terrell looked serious as he said this. Bigger than an elephant was a serious thing.

"Whoa," Shalitha said. "Bigger than an elephant. What do they look like?"

"They have colors. Some are red and some are green. That's because boy dragons are red and girl dragons are green." Terrell felt proud for knowing so much about this rare subject, and suddenly knowing things he had never known before seemed to make it even better.

"I like the green girl dragons," Shalitha said. "Do they breathe fire, too?"

"Yeah, all dragons breathe fire." He leaned over toward her, opened his mouth, and breathed heavily, as if he could also make fire.

After a while they decided they all needed lemonade, so Mom bought four big glasses, and they walked along drinking the sweet-sour drink, so nice and cold.

"Can we ride the bike things now?" Terrell asked.

"Yeah, yeah, yeah!" Shalitha said.

Dad and Mom looked at each other. "I guess we can do that," Dad said. It was really fun to ride in. Dad and Mom pedaled the two bikes, and Shalitha and Terrell sat in the back seat, watching people as they rode down the boardwalk. Other bike cars went by, and regular bikes, and they passed a lot of people.

While they were riding on the boardwalk, they passed a place with a sign that said Pladium. "Games," Terrell said. "Mom?"

After the ride, they went to the Pladium. The game Terrell really wanted to play was House of the Dead, where you get to shoot off a scary dead guy's head. But Mom saw the game and said, "I don't think so. Don't even ask to play that one." Instead, Mom let both of them play the game where you ride a motorcycle, but Shalitha crashed so often she wasn't having fun. Then Terrell played Brave Firefighters and put out fires.

When Shalitha saw that game she said, "They could put out the fire from a dragon."

Uh-oh. That look from Mom to Terrell was not a good one. "I didn't say it," he said.

When they were back out on the boardwalk, where Mom and Dad couldn't hear, Shalitha asked, "Could a fire hose put out a dragon fire?"

"Umm…" Terrell thought for a few seconds. "No, dragon fire is too hot."

"Do they make fire all the time?"

"No, when they're sleeping they're just smoky."

Shalitha went up on her toes and hopped across several boards of the boardwalk. "I wish I could see a dragon," she said. "I'd like to see one." She hopped on several more boards, then suddenly stopped and turned to her brother. "Terrell, do dragon mamas breathe fire on their babies? They could burn up their babies."

"No, they quit breathing fire then. Dragon mamas kiss their babies like real mamas."

"Oh, that's good. I'm glad they don't burn up their babies."

Terrell didn't like leaving the dragons entirely without ferociousness, so he added, "And daddy dragons make noises like lions." He scowled his face up and said, "Aaaarrrrr!" in imitation of a daddy dragon.

"Aaaarrrrr!" Shalitha said back.

"Aaaarrrrr!" said Terrell.

"Aaaarrrrr!" said Shalitha.

"These kids are growling," Dad said. "Maybe they need some lunch. How about pizza?"

"Yeah! Yeah! Yeah!" they both said. Then, just to Shalitha, Terrell said, "Dragons eat pizza, too." They had lunch in a place where it was cool inside. The walls had nets and starfish, and Dad told them what a starfish is, that it's not a real fish.

After lunch was beach time, so they went to the bathrooms on the boardwalk to change into their bathing suits, but before they left to go down to the beach, Mom got out sunscreen to rub all over them. They both hated that, but Shalitha would stand there and make a face while Mom did it. Terrell said, "Why do we have to use sunscreen? My friend Mohammed said black people don't need it."

"Oh, yeah?" Mom said. "And what medical school did your friend Mohammed go to?" Terrell knew he couldn't say anything to that, because both Mom and Dad were doctors at Jefferson in downtown Philly. "White people burn faster," Mom said, "but black people need sunscreen, too. And you're about to hold still while I put it on you." Terrell tried not to make a face like Shalitha, but he still didn't like it.

As soon as Mom and Dad would let them go, they ran across the beach toward the water, but they knew they couldn't get in yet because they just ate lunch. Dad set up an umbrella and Mom spread out towels.

"I want to dig a hole," Shalitha said, and Mom gave her a shovel for the sand. Terrell watched a guy who was flying over the water with a parachute, and he wished he could do that, too. Then he got a shovel to help Shalitha, because it was fun to dig and make a big hole, and water would come up sometimes and go in the hole. With the sand from the hole, they made a big pile until they had a mountain. Then Terrell started digging a hole in the side of the sand mountain.

"What you making?" Shalitha asked.

"This is a cave where a dragon lives."

"How can it live in there? You said it's bigger than an elephant."

"This is just a pretend dragon cave," he said. He kept digging.

"OK," she said. "I want to make a pretend dragon cave, too." She squatted down beside the sand pile and began digging in the side of it. "Do they have dragon babies in the cave?" she asked.

"Yeah, that's where dragon mamas have their babies."

"OK, I have dragon babies in my cave. Pretend dragon babies." She started singing. "Go to sleep dragon babies. Sleepy sleepy babies."

Terrell dug even deeper into the pile of sand. "There's something else dragons do," he said. "They swim in the water to catch fish, because they eat them."

"But you said they eat pizza."

"Yeah. They eat two things. Pizza and fish."

"Are you waking up, dragon babies?" Shalitha asked, kneeling down and peering into the hole she had dug. "Aaaarrrrr, your daddy's home."

"Hey, kids, nice hole." They looked up and Dad was standing there, looking at their hole full of water. "I'll show you how to make a drip castle." Dad kneeled down and took a handful of drippy wet sand out of the hole, then let the wet sand dribble down onto their sand mountain until it made a funny little pile. He took another handful and did the same thing. "If you keep doing this you'll get an interesting castle," he said.

Terrell also took some wet sand to do what Dad did. "That's it," Dad said.

"Me, too," said Shalitha, but she let the sand out too fast and it made a kind of blob.

"Good," Dad said. "Try it again, and hold your hand tighter."

They built a really good castle, and Terrell and Shalitha knew that dragons lived in the castle, but they didn't tell Dad

214

about that part. Then Dad took them down to the water, where they jumped up whenever waves came by. He held Shalitha's hands and pulled her up sometimes when the waves were too high. Terrell was too old to have Dad hold his hand when he was jumping over waves, so he jumped by himself. Some people went way out in the water, and some kids had things they were sliding on near the water, but Terrell and Shalitha liked jumping in the water with Dad. That was better.

When they came out, Dad went back to lie on a towel with Mom, and Terrell and Shalitha played some more on the beach. There were a lot of footprints going up and down the sand, so many different ones.

Terrell found a strange-looking footprint and squatted down. "I think this is a dragon footprint," he said.

Shalitha squatted down, too. "Are you sure?"

"No, I'm not sure, but I'm pretty sure. It could be. A dragon might have come down here to catch some fish. And look." He reached down and picked up a shell. "Here's a dragon toenail. So it must be a dragon footprint."

"A toenail?" Shalitha took the shell from him. "They have big toenails."

"Yeah."

"Is there more?" she asked, and began looking around.

They both began picking up dragon toenails, to get as many as they could. In a little bit, she came over to show her brother what she had found. Some of what she had was pointed shells. "Those aren't dragon toenails," he said. "The toenails are round."

"Oh," she said. She looked at the pointed ones. "But I like these, too."

When they had too many to carry in their hands, they went up to pile them on the sand next to Mom's towel.

"Did you get some nice shells?" Mom asked.

"Yeah," Terrell said. "There's a lot of them on this beach."

"We'll get a nice jar for you to put them in when we get home," Mom said. She looked at his shells, then asked, "Would yall like some ice cream?"

They forgot about shells and forgot about dragon toenails, because nothing is as good as ice cream. They walked with Mom up to the stand by the boardwalk, past a whole lot of people lying on the beach, and she bought them ice cream bars, maybe the best ice cream they had ever eaten. Terrell would only eat vanilla ice cream, but Shalitha liked any kind.

So it was a good day at the shore, like it should be. They rode the bike cars and ate pizza and played on the beach, and before they went home Mom bought them baseball caps that said Ocean City with dolphins on the front.

In the car on the way home, Terrell and Shalitha were quiet. Once in a while they whispered to each other, but mostly they just looked out the window. After a while, Mom turned around and looked at them, then said to Dad, "It looks like these kids are draggin'."

"No, we're not," Terrell said. "We're not the dragon."

Terrell and Shalitha laughed and kept laughing, and after that, everything seemed funny.

A New Piece for Cello

Isaco looked at his heart floating in the glass bottle. It seemed larger than he expected. "Tua misericordia," he said softly, a simple prayer he had been taught as a boy. *What God decides is what will be.*

"You'll be as solid as a rock once we get that in your chest," the doctor said. "Do you play a sport?"

"No," Isaco said. "I play cello."

"Oh, that's right. You're a musician on Luna, aren't you?"

"I teach cello at Armstrong University." Isaco looked again at his heart in the bottle. What a difference it was to actually do something, compared to hearing about other people's experiences. He knew a woman at the university who had received new kidneys, or the little boy of one of the secretaries, who had been blinded in an accident and got new eyes. But to do it yourself, supply the DNA, wait for the organ to grow, take a flight to Terra, head swirling with anxious thoughts, with that fear in your stomach… No, doing it yourself, in your own flesh, was nothing like hearing about it. Isaco looked back at the doctor and tried to smile.

"Don't worry," the doctor said, "we've been doing this a long time. This really is your heart, and you'll be fine." He turned to the nurse and spoke in a language Isaco didn't understand. She replied in the same language. Isaco glanced over and saw a dark-haired woman entering information on the screen.

Six months ago Isaco first noticed he was breathing harder, that it had become more difficult to draw breath. "Nothing we can really do to fix your heart," the doctor had said. Isaco stared at the doctor in shock. "It's a genetic problem, very unusual for someone as young as you," the doctor told him. "The only real solution is to give you a new heart. I'm going to send you to Princeton, in Nijersey. It's one of the best organ centers on Terra." So easy for the doctor to say. It wasn't his damaged heart beating with fear.

A week ago Isaco's friends gave him a going-off party, just after the academic term ended. Kalitrina and Isaco stood by the window of his apartment, looking at the crater wall curving to the left, with stars to the right.

"Hey, Isaco," someone had shouted across the room. "A message just came from Terra. They grew you a new ass by mistake."

Kalitrina frowned and said, "Have you noticed that John is always the first person to get drunk at a party?"

"He's stressed about applying for promotion," Isaco said. He looked back out the window. "Do you miss Terra?"

Kalitrina had gone to school on Terra for her engineering degree. "Yeah, sometimes. Of course." She turned to Isaco and smiled. "As soon as you recover from the operation, you can see some of Terra, and you'll love it, you have to. If you don't, you can't be my friend anymore." She laughed, then leaned over and kissed him on the cheek. "And you'll be fine."

"I hate to miss Kennan's recital," he said.

Kalitrina took his hand. "You'll be OK."

Only three days ago Isaco had taken the six-hour flight to Terra, landing in Kansasidy, where he first felt the amazing lead-heavy gravity. He lifted up his ponderous footsteps to catch the Transcontinental Express to Niyork, and two hours later he stepped out of the shuttle in Princeton, where he stood gaping in astonishment at the exuberance of plants, trees, grass—plants and plants and plants, everywhere he looked. No photograph could prepare you for how remarkable that was.

Isaco saw Kalitrina with other friends coming down the passage, talking with great animation. When they saw him they said, "Did you miss the show? How could you miss it?" Kalitrina came up to him and asked, "How do you feel? How do you feel? Are you comfortable?" She started to fade away and Isaco realized with surprise that he was lying on his back. He fluttered his eyes open and took a deep breath. He was on a bed in a strange room and he remembered that he was in a hospital on Terra. A woman was looking down at him. He recognized the dark-haired nurse he had seen before.

"How do you feel?" she asked.

His lips were dry and slightly stuck together. "OK," he said. "I'm thirsty."

"I thought you might be," she said. "Sip on this." She held out a cup with a straw. "Your operation went very smoothly, everything was good. The doctor will be by to talk to you later."

When he had drunk enough he nodded and she pulled the straw away. Then she smiled at him, the first smile of his life with a new heart. It was one of the sweetest smiles he had ever seen.

By the end of the week, with the help of hospital aides, he was walking slowly across the room. Various doctors, nurses, and other medical personnel came by to check on him, to ask how he was feeling. The nurse he'd seen when he first woke up came by every afternoon. She told him that her name was

Rubiya, the same name as the actress Rubiya Hannasdottir. Isaco felt pleased that this pleasant nurse had the same name as an actress he had always liked so much. He also noticed that Rubiya always wore earrings with a reddish stone.

"What are your earrings?" he asked.

"Amber," she said. "It has magical properties." He started to smile, but then stopped when she looked serious.

She also asked him questions about Luna, as she had never been there. "How much gravity do you have?" she asked. "Can you float around up there?"

"No," he said. "But it's so intense here. I wonder how you all stand it."

"I feel light as a feather," she said, and laughed. "Or I used to be light as a feather. I played a lot of zoomball in college, but those days are gone." She patted herself on the belly, then laughed again.

Hearing a voice outside the room, he asked, "What language are all the doctors and nurses speaking?"

"Mandarin," she said. "You don't speak Mandarin on Luna?"

"No, most people speak English."

"Really? Well, we speak English here in America, of course. But really? You don't speak Mandarin on Luna?" She looked very surprised. "It's the standard language on Terra."

"I guess some people know it," he said, and began to feel embarrassed.

For the next two weeks Isaco grew increasingly stronger, but in spite of watching movies, reading, or talking to his friends back on Luna, he grew terribly bored with being confined mostly to one room. The boredom disappeared, however, when Rubiya came by in the afternoons. She always took time to talk to him a bit, and she seemed truly interested in what he said. He soon began looking forward after lunch to seeing her appear at the door. One day when he expected her, waiting to tell her about his best student from two years ago, who was now performing on Terra, another woman showed up. Rubiya had taken the day off.

Isaco was surprised with how disappointed he felt, grew irritated at himself for being so foolish, told himself that she'd be back later and what difference did his little story make anyway? And then he felt disappointed and deprived the rest of the day.

The next day she was there, and again he told himself he was foolish for feeling so glad to see her. She came in with another question about life on Luna. "Does all your food grow in tanks?" she asked.

"Tanks?" he said. Where did she get such an odd idea? "Why would it grow in tanks? What would that be, like liquid or something? Our food grows in containers, like here."

"That's not like here," she said. "Most of our food grows in the ground, not in containers."

Another day she asked him how long he'd been teaching. "Eight years," he said. "I think I've gotten to be pretty good at it. I love teaching the cello. I just can't imagine doing anything else." He leaned a bit forward in his chair. "Do you like the cello? It has such a tone, like…angels' voices." He frowned faintly, afraid that his simile had sounded stupid.

"I love the cello," she said. "What kind of training did you have to have? Can you play other instruments?"

"Oh, sure. I play viola and violin, but not as well, and the piano. But the cello, that's…that's—" He sighed contentedly without realizing it. "The cello is my reason. I wanted to play cello since I was eight years old."

"So you always knew," she said. "When I was young I wanted to be a marine biologist, but there was too much math. So I became a nurse." She made an odd, slightly dopey expression, perhaps the expression of someone weak in math. "It would be nice to hear you play the cello," she said.

"I wish I could do that." He smiled and said, "I have a musician joke for you. I don't know if non-musicians can appreciate these jokes. Why are orchestra intermissions limited to twenty minutes?" He smiled broadly. "So you don't have to retrain the drummers." He laughed and Rubiya laughed along with him. "One of my students told me that one," he said.

After three weeks Isaco was moved into a patient apartment, where he would live for a while longer but more independently. Rubiya said she would come by after work and visit him. The very day he moved in, she was there later in the day, a little to his surprise, and he felt very happy and flattered that she had come by so quickly. They talked that evening for an hour, and Isaco told her about his father, who was a chef for a hotel in Copernicus, where people went to see the famous light shows.

"I'm not really that close to him, though," Isaco said. "He and my mother divorced when I was three. We got a lot of presents, but we didn't see him much. Mama was the first one to teach me to play the piano. She raised me and my two brothers."

"What do your brothers do?" Rubiya asked.

"Matt's a lawyer. But Ilyon..." He sighed heavily. "Ilyon never really has worked. He's a smart guy, but his brain is going to waste. He plays a lot of games." Isaco's expression darkened and he grew silent for a moment. Then he looked at Rubiya and asked, "Do you have brothers or sisters?"

"No," she said. "It's just me and Mammu. I had a brother when I was really young, but when I was three he drowned."

"I'm sorry," Isaco said.

"A long time ago," she said, but then she was silent for several seconds. "He was just ten years old and swam out too far in the ocean. Nobody was really sure exactly what happened, because he was a good swimmer."

"It must have been hard to lose your brother."

"Yes," she said, "but I was pretty young. You know, really, I think a lot of my memories of him are fake memories, things I heard about him when I got older. But I'm close to Mammu now. Her health isn't good and I take care of her." Again there was a silence, then she said, "In another week you can start going out on excursions if you want. They encourage it, in fact. How would you like a local guide?"

"As long as it's you," he said. He smiled at her. "I'll tell you about Luna in exchange. How we float around and drink our food out of tanks."

"Huh, well, if you're going to make fun of me."

"Oh no! I'm joking. I didn't—"

"I know," she said, then laughed. "I'd love to show you around."

Exactly a week later she took him for a ride through Princeton. As they drove, Rubiya was delighted to watch Isaco react to what was so familiar to her, like naked children on the playgrounds. "Clothes are so expensive," she said. "And why do children need to wear clothes anyway in good weather?" Or so much green, so many plants. Even if there was just one centimeter of soil between a wall and a sidewalk, a plant would be growing there.

"What keeps them from just taking over everything?" he asked. "They seem to grow everywhere."

"They do take over everything," she said. "If you let them. We have to cut them back. But you're lucky to be here in May. This is one of the prettiest months."

"My God," he said. "Tua misericordia." Entire trees full of flowers, a landscape full of flowers. What a universe of miracles God had fashioned.

When they got out of the vehicle for a short walk to see a row of azaleas, Rubiya looked shocked to see Isaco react with wide-eyed fear to a squirrel. When they got back in the vehicle, he asked what the creature was. She told him and said she could understand that he might not have seen a squirrel before, living on Luna. But then he asked, "How did it get loose?"

"Get loose?" she asked.

"From wherever it was kept."

"It's not kept anywhere," she said. "It lives in the park."

"You let animals run around loose?" he asked. He had an expression that looked distrustful, as if she were making this up.

"Haven't you ever read about Terra?" she asked.

"Of course I have," he said, a little offended. "But mostly about the music. I was never very interested in biology."

"This is a normal planet," she said. "Animals live here. Most of them are free to go where they want."

He missed the implication that Luna was not normal, as a large insect landed on the window he was looking out of. He recoiled slightly, but tried not to let Rubiya see it, then turned to her and said, "I'll get used to it, then. I'd like to see more, if my guide isn't giving up."

She reached out and put her hand on top of his. "You are such a brave boy," she said. "Would you like to see food growing? There's a lot of agriculture here in Nijersey."

He rolled his hand over so that their palms were together. "I want to see everything," he said. She squeezed his hand.

She showed him fields of tomatoes, fields of beans, orchards of peach trees in bloom. Then two weeks later the doctors judged that Isaco had recovered enough to take longer trips, and when she had a day off Rubiya took him on a day trip to Bangkok. "We'll see Buddhist temples," she said, temples that she wanted to see again herself, and of course the food, ahh, the food. Rubyia, it turned out, was a gourmet cook, and she appreciated a wide variety of cuisines. When they arrived in Bangkok they went to the Wat Arun Buddhist temple, where Isaco admired the astonishing ornate spires, like a tourist. Rubiya sat for a while to meditate while he walked around.

Later, when they began to think about lunch, she led him away from the first place he looked at, a Senegalese restaurant. "I like them," she said. "I'm just tired of them now. They're everywhere. Every place you go there's always a Senegalese restaurant." Instead they chose a local Thai place, where they had lunch sitting at an outdoor terrace, looking at the Jao Praya River. Rubiya talked to the waiter in Mandarin to order. Isaco ate

233

the unfamiliar but delicious food, intently watching birds fly over the river. After several minutes he said aloud, but to himself, "People used to watch birds like this." He said it as a discovery, something so simple, so obvious, but he had never thought about this before. "They watched birds and wanted to fly. That's why I live on Luna." He felt as though he had come back to watch the origin of history. Sitting here in this remarkable city, eating this strange food, across from Rubiya, he was filled with discovery and life and happiness.

"I have a musician joke for you," he said. "You have to understand conductors maybe. What's the difference between God and a conductor?" He waited to give his punch line. "God knows he's not a conductor." He laughed and Rubiya smiled. "Or here's another. How can you tell when a violist is playing out of tune? The bow is moving." He laughed and she laughed with him.

When they left the restaurant she said, "You know, I still want to hear you play."

He stopped and turned toward her. "And I would love to play for you." He hesitated three seconds, then put his arms around her and kissed her, as she kissed him back. Afterward they stood for a moment, arms around one another, her head on his chest, as they breathed together, feeling one another's heartbeat.

When they continued walking, their arms around each other's waist, he asked, "Can I get a cello?"

"I'll find out," she said.

"You know, I always joke with my students about playing an instrument that's so much trouble to carry around. It would be nice to just stick it in your pocket, like a piccolo player."

Every day after work she came by his apartment, where they talked about music, about fruits that grew only in certain African valleys, or about God and Buddha, and they traded kisses that melted all the earth away into nothingness.

One day they went to Paris. Watching children sail boats in the fountain of the Luxembourg Gardens, with Rubiya beside him, holding his arm, the feel of her there against him was so perfectly right that Isaco felt astounded by the glory of life. He felt like he had found a second reason for being born and realized he couldn't imagine being away from her. It wasn't just enjoying her company. He needed her now.

"I'm in love with you," he said.

She turned to him, looked at him seriously.

"I just realized it," he said.

"But I already knew it," she told him. "And I'm in love with you." She laughed and looked happy. "I love you, Luna boy."

Two days after Paris, Rubiya took Isaco down to her own house in Millville, to meet her mother and see how a normal person lived on Terra. Rubiya's mother was sitting on the couch when they arrived, and Rubiya said, "You don't have to get up, Mammu. Here he is. This is Isaco."

To avoid the awkwardness of standing over Rubiya's mother, Isaco quickly sat on the couch beside her. She took his hand and said, "And he's such a good-looking boy." He smiled slightly, but blushed. "I'm glad Rubiya finally brought you down."

"I'm very happy to meet you," he said. "You have a beautiful place here."

"I love to garden but can't do that much anymore."

"Mammu, you want a cup of tea?" Rubiya asked.

"Yes, I guess I need to take a pill." She turned back to Isaco. "How are *you* feeling?" she asked. "How was your operation?"

Later in the afternoon, Isaco watched Rubiya ride a horse in the field behind the house. He knew she would not be doing this if it was really dangerous, but it definitely looked dangerous, sitting on top of a large animal as it ran. It looked crazy, in fact. "It's great," Rubyia yelled as she galloped by.

"You're going to learn to do this." He was pretty sure that would never ever happen.

When she came down from the enormous animal, Rubiya said, "I have something you'll like much more."

He put his arms around her and asked, "It wouldn't be a million kisses, would it? I'd like that better."

"Oh, well...yes," she said, and went soft against him as he kissed her. When she finally pulled her lips away, he stroked and kissed her hair. Eventually she said, "But there's still something else in the house."

They went inside, and in a back room she showed him a large black case. "I rented a cello."

"Oh," he said. He opened the case and looked at the reddish wood, touched the smooth top of the instrument, then plucked a string. Suddenly he recalled how it felt to be with his students, that feeling of wanting to give them something. "Let's see how it sounds," he said. That evening he played for Rubiya and her mother, played Pachelbel's "Canon in D", an excerpt from Handel's "Water Music", the conclusion of "Wandering Truth" by Karl Dlamini, and a piece he had written himself, "Late Passage".

"That's so wonderful," Rubiya's mother said.

"It sounds even better on my own cello," he said. "I need to get my cello."

That night, after Rubiya had gotten her mother to bed, she and Isaco sat in old chairs outside under the trees. They were drinking a bottle of red wine from Mozambique, looking up at the whiteness of Luna, round and full above them.

"It's so strange to see your home like that," he said, looking at the moon.

They sat silently for a few minutes, then Rubiya said what he already knew. "I can't go there. I can't leave Mammu."

"I know," Isaco said. "No, I know that. I'll come here. If this is where you are, this is where I'll be. I'm sure universities here have cello teachers. I can have students here."

"Oh, Isaco," she said. She sounded unhappy. "I wish you knew more about Terra. It's illegal for you to work here."

"What? How can it be illegal? Against the law to work?"

"Lunans can move here, but it's illegal to work." She leaned over and took his hands. "I know how much the teaching means to you. And I can't ask you to give it up for me. But that's the law here. It's because unemployment is so high on Terra. You can come here and get Public Payments to live on, but you can't work. They even encourage Terrans to give up their jobs and live on Public Payments, to free up jobs for other people."

He opened his mouth, but his feelings didn't turn into words, and he slowly closed it again.

"Say something," Rubiya said.

"Teaching is my life," he said.

She moved to sit in his lap and held her face against his. He felt wetness on his cheek and knew she was crying. He wanted to cry with her.

Eventually, he said, "I need to take a walk."

She leaned back slightly and looked at him.

He said, "Can I just... I need to walk and think."

"Should I walk with you?" she asked.

"Let me have a few minutes by myself." He wanted to smile at her, but instead he suddenly hugged her tightly, then stood. Only seconds before, life had seemed to be moving into a perfect arrangement. Life can trick you that way.

For a week afterward he felt a heaviness that marred his joy, and at the end of that week he called Kalitrina on Luna.

"Isaco, I've been thinking of calling you," she said. "Have you set a date for a Registration Ceremony with Rubiya?"

"What?" he said, somewhat stunned. "Did she call you?"

"No. She didn't need to call me. Aren't you in love with her? Isn't it the logical thing to do? You are going to get registered, right?"

"How do you know this?" he asked.

"Honey, you do know about the X-Y chromosome thing, don't you? I'm a woman. Haven't I been talking to you for the last few weeks?"

"But I don't—"

"Have you set a date?"

"No, not yet."

"Well, you know I'm going to be there."

"Kalitrina, I won't be able to work here."

"Not legally, anyway," she said.

"I'll have to give up teaching. I wonder if I can do it."

"Isaco, am I hearing the man I know? Is there too much oxygen up there for you? How many times did you sit in my apartment and complain about not having enough time to work on your own composing?"

"I did say that."

"Frequently. So now you have someone you love, someone you want to get registered with, and you'll have time to compose. Did you call me to tell me how happy you are?"

*

A breeze blew, pushing hair into Rubiya's face, and she reached up to move it. Isaco ignored the breeze, concentrating on the movements of his bow, as the music grew faster, then faster still. They were on the back porch of their house, and he was playing her a new composition he had written.

When he finished she held both hands over her heart, then moved her hands toward him, opening up so that her fingers pointed to him. "What is it called?" she asked.

"I don't know," he said. "It doesn't have a name yet."

The Orchid House

When Lucy's husband, Mitch, was working as a prison guard, he and Larry would go to Jackson's bar next to the prison. With those rolls of barbed wire just across the street, Mitch and Larry would drink beer and talk about how they wished it was already deer-hunting season. If it *was* already deer-hunting season, they'd talk about how they wished they had more time to go to the woods. Mitch never actually hunted very much, and when he died of cirrhosis, that didn't make the world a lot safer for the deer. Lucy used the insurance money to attend a business college for a degree as a clinical medical assistant and to take a vacation to Ft. Lauderdale. Now she works for a podiatrist who has an office up on the hill near the hospital.

All of this information about Lucy is in a gray notebook, written down by Howell George, who rents a house out in the country from Lucy. Howell works as a part-time religion professor at the college in Huntingdon, where Lucy lives with her mother. Howell is one of the many people who say they "want to be a writer", so he imagines that he is going to do it one day, write something, and he keeps notebooks full of possibly useful information. The notes on Lucy are part of that possibly useful information, and well, maybe. Maybe Howell will want to write about a character like her someday. Then he can just look in that notebook to see that Lucy lives with her mother, Clara, who she is very close to, that Lucy appears to be in her mid-thirties, and that she dislikes dogs so much she will not allow renters to have them. Lucy's last name is Sweet, which she told Howell is her married name. "A prison guard named Sweet," she said. "The prisoners must have loved that. Cause he wasn't, exactly."

Howell is originally from Allentown, in eastern Pennsylvania but has spent much of his professional life teaching religion in the central part of the state, working temporarily at various colleges. In the office at the college where he teaches now, he has a poster of Shiva dancing, one leg lifted high, multiple arms waving in the air, and surrounded by a circle of flames. Destruction leads into creation, as Shiva brings about the transformation of life. At home Howell has a small ceramic statue of the same image, dancing transformation on the kitchen windowsill. Howell is fascinated by ideas that show a connection between apparent contradictions in life. He likes his current job, and he sees it as his educational mission to get students to embrace the inexplicable complexity of the world. They don't always want to do that.

The house where Howell lives is ten miles from the town where he teaches. The road isn't heavily traveled, but enough traffic goes by that Howell would not want his dog to run freely in the yard, if he had a dog, but he doesn't, because Lucy won't allow dogs in the house he is renting. The white wooden house isn't large, though it has two stories with a front porch. A week after Howell moves in, Lucy comes out to look at the refrigerator. While she's there she tells him that a married couple, DeWitt and Cynthia Horvath, in their forties, live in the dark yellow house next door. Lucy says DeWitt can be kind of intense, but Cynthia is nice.

"What do you mean intense?" Howell asks.

"Oh, well," Lucy says and waves her hand toward the yellow house, then turns away from it. "He threatened to kill somebody." She takes out a piece of gum and unwraps it. "Did I tell you I just quit smoking a week ago? I don't know if I can live through this."

"To kill somebody?" Howell looks at Lucy, then toward the yellow house.

"I don't think he meant it," she says. She turns back to Howell, smiles, and blinks several times quickly, something he has seen her do before. "I mean he's alright," she says. "He's not dangerous or anything." Howell is thinking that Lucy is rather cute when she smiles, and she's not much older than him, maybe thirty-four or thirty-five, but thinking about dating brings his old girlfriend Riva to mind.

"If you need anything," Lucy tells him before she leaves, "don't worry about calling. I don't mind if you call." She smiles at him again, a very friendly smile, he thinks.

After Lucy tells Howell about the Horvaths next door, he plans to introduce himself when he sees them in the yard, but that doesn't happen soon. A few times early in the morning, when Howell is standing in his kitchen with a cup of coffee, thinking how unfortunate it is that each day has to begin first thing in the morning, he sees DeWitt go out to his green pickup truck. On the back of the truck is a horizontal wooden pole, and a flag with a picture of a flower is attached, so wherever DeWitt drives that flower is flapping behind him. Eventually Howell gets his chance. He comes home from the supermarket and finds DeWitt and Cynthia sitting in their back yard in lawn chairs. It seems like a good time, so Howell walks over. DeWitt is wearing shorts and an open shirt, and Cynthia has on a light cotton dress printed with orange flowers. Between their lawn chairs is a small metal table, with two glasses on it.

"Hey," Howell says. "I'm a new kid in the neighborhood and thought I'd come over and say hello."

"How are you?" DeWitt says and sits up straight, as if he will get up. He's very balding from the front, and he looks like a pleasant guy. Not like someone who would threaten to kill a person. "We're just having our afternoon cocktail, gin and tonic. Can I get you one?"

"Thanks," Howell answers. "I'll sure take you up another time, but I've got to go soon to meet somebody in Altoona."

"You just moved in, didn't you?" Cynthia asks. She smiles at Howell and he thinks she gives him a little wave, but she's just brushing away a fly.

"I moved in in August," Howell says.

"Too hot to move then," she says. She half smiles and slightly rolls her eyes, then reaches for her drink.

Her husband leans back into his chair and says, "Oh yeah. You're right, sweetie." He laughs. "It was a hot bastard back in August." He reaches over and picks up his own glass.

"Yeah, it was hot," Howell says. "I definitely want to join you folks for a drink another time, but I'm headed for Altoona in a little bit. Oh, well, I just said that."

It's only later, as he's driving his own pickup truck down the mountain toward Altoona, that it strikes Howell why he felt a slight but strange emotion with Cynthia Horvath. She had made an odd expression that reminded him of Riva, his ex-girlfriend. Riva left Howell two years ago, and he still yearns for her. As he is driving down the mountain, he recalls his most powerful memory of her. He woke once in the middle of the night to find she was not in bed, but he heard her voice. He got up and left the bedroom to find her on the stairs, standing in the dark next to a window. In the moonlight through the window her pale nightgown stood out in the darkness. What makes this memory still bring tears to Howell's eyes is that as Riva stood there in the moonlight on the stairs, she was singing "I Will Always Love You". It turned out, though, that she didn't always love him.

He has been without her now for two years, but he continues to hope that they might get back together, and once in a while they talk on the phone. Howell carries his hopeless dream the way most people do, ignoring the facts as much as possible, occasionally thinking of similar cases where patience has been rewarded, and frequently drifting down the sweet river of fantasy, where everything happens the way it ought to. If he just gives Riva enough time, if he's thoughtful and patient with her, eventually she'll realize how good they were together and come back.

He is thinking of her one day almost unconsciously, letting her drift into his mind, as he walks across the college campus to the library. When he steps inside the small library, he glances to the right and thinks *Is that Lucy?* Did he just see his landlady go into a stack of books? Howell turns in the direction where he thinks Lucy went.

It is Lucy. He finds her at the back of the library, holding an open book and looking at it. She's standing near the medical reference books.

"I thought that was you," he says. She looks up, a little surprised, solemn, more serious than he's seen her before.

"Hello, Howell," she says. "Why are you here?"

"I just came over to turn a book in," he replies.

"Oh," Lucy says. He expects her to say more, but she doesn't. He sees that she is slowly chewing gum, still very serious looking.

"So you want to check a book out?" he asks.

She looks down at the book she's holding. "I don't know. Maybe. If they'll..." She looks down at her book and stops speaking.

Howell sees that things are not alright with Lucy, but even so he asks, "Are you alright?"

"Mama has cancer," Lucy says.

Howell isn't sure how to reply to this, and he knows he's not good with this kind of thing. "Do you want to sit down?" he asks and indicates the small couch nearby. Lucy nods yes and walks over to sit, and Howell sits beside her.

"I've been trying to get her to go to the doctor, and she finally went. He said she has endometrial cancer." Lucy doesn't say anything for a moment, then adds, "Goddamnit, I want a cigarette. Fucking chewing gum is not a substitute."

Howell is sitting so close to Lucy on the tiny couch that he almost has to make an effort not to sit up against her. In the space between them she has her hand on the couch, and he has a strong feeling of wanting to put his hand on top of hers, but he doesn't. "When are they going to start treatment?" he asks.

"No. No." Lucy shakes her head. "We're not going to get into that chemotherapy stuff. They just mess you up with that. I'm gonna research alternative treatments, herbal stuff, acupuncture, I don't know. And Mama can do spiritual healing.

253

We heard about some of those things when I was studying to be a medical assistant."

Howell feels disturbed by what Lucy is saying, which sounds extreme to him. But she looks up at him, and now she doesn't look so hopeless and scared. Now she looks ready to argue for her point of view, maybe to fight for her mother's life. Again he wants to put his hand on top of hers, he can even feel the nervous impulses wanting to lift his arm, but still he doesn't do it.

Later that week Howell sees Lucy at the grocery store, and she tells him that she went to Sweet Annie Herbs downtown and bought red clover for Clara. Howell has been by the big old house where the herb shop is located, but he's never been in, and he doesn't know anything at all about herbal supplements. A couple of weeks afterward, when he's talking to DeWitt, Howell tells him about Clara using red clover. Howell says he doesn't understand how somebody could refuse treatment for cancer. They're talking in the small greenhouse DeWitt has built back behind his house, where he grows orchids. They each have a beer from the refrigerator DeWitt also has in the greenhouse.

"There's some cancers you can cure," Howell says. "But there's none of them you can cure if you don't treat it."

"She's treating it with the herbal stuff," DeWitt says. He finishes off the beer he's drinking, drops the bottle in a recycle bucket, and takes another from the refrigerator.

"People who do that, I think they call them dead," Howell says.

"No, no, some of that herbal stuff is good, it works. All drugs came from plants to start with."

"Yeah," Howell says, "but I think doctors know more than that now."

"I'm sure they do, but chemotherapy really fucks you up, hair falling out, puking." DeWitt goes to a fan mounted in a corner of the tiny greenhouse and turns it on.

"Why do you run a fan?" Howell asks.

"Orchids do better with moving air," DeWitt says. He leans over one of the plants heavy with purple-and-white blossoms. "Oh, man, look at this beauty. I've gotta get Cynthia out here to look at this. She'll love this." He looks up at Howell and says, "Do you need another beer? Or we could go in the house and I could make us some real drinks. How about a screwdriver?"

They leave the greenhouse and shuffle through the deep autumn leaves back to the house. DeWitt says it'll be a cold day in hell before he rakes leaves living out in the country. In the last few weeks Howell and DeWitt have become very friendly, and Howell enjoys going over to drink with him. From their conversations they've learned a lot about one another. Now DeWitt knows that Howell wants to retire to Mexico, even though he doesn't speak Spanish, that a few years ago he used to sneak into a neighbor's yard to go skinny dipping in their pool, that he hates cell phones and swears he'll never have one, and that he saw a UFO once, and seriously, it wasn't just some cloud formation. And Howell knows that DeWitt believes George Jones was sent here by God to record albums, that once in downtown Pittsburgh at two in the morning DeWitt made love to Cynthia in the backseat of their car, that every year he and Cynthia go on vacation to Myrtle Beach, and that he wishes the goddamned white-tailed deer were extinct because he's hit so many with his truck. Also Howell has learned that DeWitt didn't exactly threaten to kill someone, just told a neighbor if he kept letting his dog shit in DeWitt's yard, DeWitt was going to shoot the dog and then shoot the neighbor. "But I wouldn't really shoot a dog," DeWitt said and laughed.

While they are drinking to excess, DeWitt offers Howell some whole-grain cookies with dates. One thing they agree on is eating healthy—whole grains, fresh local vegetables, lean venison, also local. In late October, when the Healthy Harvest Festival comes along in Huntingdon, it's the kind of thing they will both be likely to show up at, maybe to buy some local cheese or honey.

When the festival arrives, it's set up on Washington Street, which is closed off, but the 5K Run is over by Flag Pole Hill, for anyone nuts enough to want to run five kilometers at 8:30 in the morning. Howell comes into town around eleven o'clock, to check out what's going on and then go over to Boxers for lunch. He walks along looking at the booths set along the side of the street. A woman standing behind a table covered with jars of honey delightedly greets a friend walking up. A very young couple walks by, the man with a baseball cap pulled down low, the woman with a baby in a pouch on her chest. In one of the booths along the street, a woman sitting beside a spinning wheel is carding flax. In another booth a table is covered with jars of massage oil.

Howell continues to walk in the bright October sunshine, until two blocks down the street he sees a table set up under a tarp. Lucy is sitting at the table, wearing her white coat, with a stethoscope in her ears, measuring a woman's blood pressure. As Howell comes off the street Lucy glances up, sees him, and a quick smile flashes, then she looks down again, seriously listening to the faint thump of blood pounding in the middle-aged woman's arm. When Lucy has finished, she tells the woman her blood pressure is 170 over 110, which means nothing to the woman, who doesn't look the least concerned. "You should go and see your doctor about this," Lucy says.

The woman stares back with no expression, then asks, "Is it good?"

"No," Lucy says, and glances over at Howell. He is looking in surprise at the woman, who could be dead in six months. "No, it's too high," Lucy tells her. "You need to get this blood pressure down."

"I don't feel nothing," the woman says.

When the woman leaves, Howell says, "Enjoy your work?"

"We're trying to save lives here," Lucy replies. She begins to straighten up stacks of pamphlets lying on the table in front of her. Howell looks at her and thinks what pretty hands she has. She could be one of those TV hand models, showing off jewelry or soap or something.

"Maybe you could save my life," he says. "Take my blood pressure."

She looks at him and blinks several times. "Does yours need saving?" She smiles and when Howell smiles back at her, she slightly tilts her head to the right.

"I've always needed saving," he replies. "Ask anybody in my family." He rolls up his sleeve and lays his arm on the table. Lucy wraps the pressure cuff around his arm and pumps it up, then holds the diaphragm of the stethoscope against the bend of his arm. Her other hand is lying over his wrist, and Howell likes the feeling.

In a moment Lucy looks up at him and says, "Whatever you need saving from, it's not high blood pressure."

"Yeah, that's true," he says. She takes the cuff off his arm, and he asks, "How's your mom?"

Lucy nods her head a few times without speaking. "Well…" She nods again. "She's holding on. She's taking the red clover, and we found a man who comes by to do spiritual healing with her. I mean the church is praying for her, but it's more than that. I heard the clover is good for the kind of cancer she has."

"I hope so," Howell says seriously. He certainly doesn't feel hopeful of this, which seems like faith in magic to him. "I hope she'll be alright," he says.

"Thanks," Lucy says.

"Hey!" a loud voice booms out. "Is this the booth where you measure the sexual quotient?" Howell looks around to see DeWitt and Cynthia. "I need mine measured." DeWitt is grinning.

"No he doesn't," Cynthia says, and DeWitt looks at her and laughs.

"Just blood pressure here," Lucy replies. "You want your blood pressure measured?" DeWitt sits down and Lucy wraps the cuff around his arm. Before pumping it up, she looks at a place on his arm. "Have you always had this mole?" she asks.

"Long as I can remember."

"Uh huh. You just have to be careful about those things. They can turn into cancer. You spend much time in the sun?"

"Hell yeah. We go to Myrtle Beach every year." DeWitt turns to look at Cynthia and grins.

The rest of the day Howell keeps thinking about the feel of Lucy's hand on his arm. Or he's partly thinking about it, remembering how she looked bending over with the stethoscope, and partly he isn't thinking so much as experiencing a sensory memory. That feeling comes to him when he's watching a video that evening, as the memory of Lucy checking his blood pressure distracts him from the movie. The subject of memory comes up later when he's having drinks with Cynthia and DeWitt. Cynthia tells the two men that babies form memories while they're still in the womb. As she's talking, she's embroidering on a piece of white cloth, creating a picture of the British Parliament building. She goes on to say that the reason people get into the fetal position when they're upset is because they remember how peaceful it was back when they were in that position all the time. Hmm, DeWitt says, maybe, maybe, but he doesn't seem too convinced. It's true, Cynthia repeats, and she tells him that people just don't know that's what they're remembering, but DeWitt says, in that case, how does she know. Then DeWitt starts talking about a guy he read about in New England somewhere, or maybe in Belgium, who couldn't create new memories. If you met the guy he'd seem normal, hey, how you doing, like you do with a new person, but if you went out of the room and came back, he'd think he was meeting you the first time just a few minutes later.

DeWitt thinks this is one of the most horrible things he's ever heard of, being unable to make memories. He says, "Everything about us is our memory, everything that ever happened, who we know, what we know, what we know how to do, it's all memory. Since this guy can't make memories, it's the same thing as if he doesn't exist." Then DeWitt gets up for another bottle of wine.

"Get the shiraz," Cynthia says. She ties off the dark brown thread and cuts it, then lays the wooden hoop with the cloth in her lap and bends the fingers of both hands in and out. "My fingers get sore," she says. "I had a checkup today and even asked the doctor if I might be getting arthritis."

"What did he say?" Howell asks.

"He said no. But maybe it's just his job to make me feel better."

"It's his job to keep you well."

"He made me feel better about this mole, too." She points to the calf of her right leg. "I got to thinking about Lucy telling DeWitt to be careful, so I asked the doctor to take a look at mine. But it's nothing, like they usually are."

Two hours later, Howell walks back to his own house, belly full of wine and mind full of memories. Now he's already remembering sitting there with DeWitt and Cynthia. Just three minutes ago, and now that's already a memory. Another memory comes back to him as he steps into his kitchen. He and Riva used to take a bottle of wine and walk down to the river, keeping the bottle inside a picnic basket so no one would see it. Then they'd sit in the warmth of the sun, sometimes talking, sometimes without speaking, hearing the water flow by, and it felt so good to be together. Those days are certainly gone. Normally Howell can deal with the old memories, but as he recalls how contented and fulfilled he felt with Riva by the river, he suddenly feels the loss as if he's been hit in the stomach. He closes his eyes and leans his head up against the refrigerator, drawing deep breaths. DeWitt said it would be horrible to have no memories, but did he think about the fact that some memories are not good to have? To try to empty his mind and calm himself, Howell begins a Buddhist chant that he uses sometimes: *Om mani padme hum, om mani padme hum.* He does this for a few minutes, gradually standing up straight and leaning back against the refrigerator. As his mind relaxes, he thinks about the chant, about the fact that every word has an "m". Now he is breathing calmly, and he decides there must be something comforting about the sound of "m". The sound is made with the lips closed, vibrating the column of air that runs from the lips down into the chest, down to the center of the body.

Howell wouldn't call himself a Buddhist, but he leans toward it more than any other religion. Sometimes he has advised his sister to try Buddhism, because she worries too much, but Katie has always stuck with being a Catholic. For her, religion means wafers and wine and telling someone in a booth what you think you've done wrong. Still, as Christmas approaches, Howell decides to send his sister a book on Buddhism, because he thinks she needs to stop beating her head against life, needs to find another job.

On a cold sunny day, three weeks before Christmas, he drives downtown and mails the book. As he is coming down the steps of the post office he's surprised to see Cynthia walking by.

266

"Cynthia," he calls, and walks more quickly down the steps. She stops and looks up, then smiles to see him.

"Hi, Howell," she says.

"You guys ready for Christmas?" Howell asks.

"Oh. Yeah," she says, without much enthusiasm, and the smile is quickly gone. "Our minds aren't really on the holiday. I've got to have surgery tomorrow."

"Surgery?" He frowns at hearing this.

She looks quite serious now. "I was seeing my gynecologist and he noticed the mole on my leg, and he sent me to a dermatologist. They said I've got melanoma. The other doctor misdiagnosed it."

"Oh," Howell says. As with Lucy's news about her mother's cancer, he doesn't know just what to say. "Oh," he repeats.

"Yeah, so I'm having surgery to have it removed. I decided I'd try some of the herbal remedies too, since Lucy Sweet said they're working for her mother. I was just down at

267

Sweet Annie's Herb Shop. I looked on the Internet to see what to use."

"I'm sorry to hear about this," Howell tells her. "I hope the surgery goes well."

"Thanks. All I can do is hope for the best." She smiles with her mouth, but not with her eyes. "I'm sure it'll be OK."

"Yeah," he says.

Howell walks on to his truck and turns to look back at Cynthia, but she's turned the corner. He stands beside the truck for a moment. Lucy's mother, and now Cynthia.

When he gets home he stands in the kitchen, thinking about Cynthia. He leans against the sink and begins thinking about his sister, about his mother, about Riva, about Lucy. For a long time he stands with his thoughts wandering in various directions: his mother has a little dog that has epilepsy, his sister complains about her job writing for a chamber of commerce... He thinks about hugging them, then he thinks of hugging Riva, then hugging Lucy. Maybe it's Howell that wants a hug, but he's not the one who is sick.

In the next few weeks DeWitt looks pale and stern whenever Howell sees him, and Cynthia begins to wear a scarf. DeWitt no longer invites Howell over, but they still talk when they see one another.

"They say chemotherapy is pretty advanced these days," DeWitt says. "We're pretty hopeful. It's still hard on her, though. Her hair's falling out, and she has trouble keeping food down."

"I'm thinking good thoughts for her," Howell tells him.

"Yeah," DeWitt says, looking off at his yard, and he seems not to be listening now. "Yeah, good thoughts."

When Cynthia dies, the funeral is on a Thursday, at a funeral home instead of a church, and Howell takes off in the afternoon to go. Entering the hall where the service is being held, he sees Cynthia's closed casket at the front, with a mass of flowers on top of the lid. He also sees DeWitt in a gray suit sitting on the front row, next to a man who is leaning over to say something to him. Lucy is sitting halfway back from the front, but the seats around her are already filled, so Howell sits farther back. After the service, the casket is wheeled out, and DeWitt walks slowly out behind it. He looks beaten, he looks tragic, but he also looks calm.

After the casket passes, people rise to leave the hall, and Howell waits until Lucy comes back. They look at one another, nod slightly without speaking. He turns beside her to walk out together. When they leave the building, standing in the wind that has come up, Lucy says, "Oh, I'm so sorry for DeWitt." Then she turns to Howell, holding on to the small black hat she is wearing, and asks, "Are you going out to the gravesite?"

"I really need to get back to the school," he says. "But I thought I'd come down for the funeral."

"Yeah, I've got to get back to work, too," she says. They wait awkwardly for a moment, then Lucy says, "I know this doesn't seem like the right time to tell you this, but I've got the

270

wood to redo your dining room floor. I've just got to figure out how to get it over there."

"Where is it?" Howell asks.

"On my porch."

"Why don't I just come pick it up? It'll probably fit in my truck."

They agree that Howell will come by Lucy's house later to pick up the wood, and then Lucy will follow him out to where he lives to look at the dining room. A few hours later he arrives at Lucy's house and spends about thirty minutes loading the wood. He also talks to Lucy's mother, who is feeling well and swears by the herbal supplement she is taking.

As Howell is driving out of town, with Lucy following, they are coming around a curve approaching the tavern on the right when a green truck flies past them in the other lane, headed back toward town. Howell looks over in surprise and a little anger at what he thinks is reckless driving, then is shocked to realize there was a flag flying from a pole on the back of the truck. *Wasn't that DeWitt?*

A minute later Howell drives faster himself, as he sees the light of a fire ahead. He speeds up until he can pull into his driveway, and without even turning off the engine, gets out and stands amazed. DeWitt's house is on fire. The flames have already started to engulf the entire structure, rising up to crackle above the second floor. Then Howell sees the greenhouse in the backyard, where DeWitt grows orchids. DeWitt has smashed all the glass in the greenhouse. Howell wonders if he should go after him.

Now Lucy has parked and is standing beside Howell, and for this moment they stand and stare incredulously at the sight. "Oh, my God," Lucy says, then she turns toward Howell as he puts his arms around her and pulls her close to him. In turn she wraps her arms around his back, and they stand embracing one another.

✸

The Way We Feel in Sunlight

The butterfly in Johnny's most famous painting had moved into the dark area of the picture. The wings, however, were lit by a beam of sunlight, making the figure of the insect stand out. Museums across the country now owned paintings he'd done, and even many critics said good things about him. In the famous painting with the butterfly he had portrayed his niece, Addie— his sister Leah's daughter. Addie was slightly plump, with black hair down to her shoulders and a sly smile. She was nineteen now, but mentally she was still about three years old. She would never live on her own, or care. The picture "Floating in Sunlight" showed Addie at fifteen, sitting on the ground, head back, laughing at the butterfly. The figure of Addie was flooded with a warm light, set off by a dark background around her. Johnny had eventually realized that all of his paintings of Addie were intended to make her okay, and every painting of her was positive in one way or another.

But now Addie's mother, Leah, was dying. Johnny had just been visiting her, and as he arrived home, walking up to his porch, he heard a high girlish voice say, "I'm playing with Jojo." He looked off the porch and in the yard saw his neighbor's child, Marlianna, who was four years old. She was standing by the red and yellow cosmos flowers that Johnny had planted, now blooming out for summer.

"Hello, Marlianna," he said.

"Hey, Johnny," she said. She grinned at him. "I'm playing with Jojo."

There was no one with her, so Johnny guessed Jojo must be next door in Marlianna's yard. "Maybe Jojo's in your yard looking for you," he said.

"No, Jojo's right here. He's invisible." Johnny had long ago lost any feeling that there might be magic in the world, as he was now in his mid-fifties, so he was surprised to hear his little neighbor say this.

Marlianna came up the steps to the porch. "Guess where we went," she said. She was smiling and began swinging back and forth, holding on to one of the round posts that held up the porch roof.

"With Jojo?"

"No," she said. "Jojo wouldn't go. With my mama."

"I give up," Johnny said.

"You can't give up," she said. She stopped swinging and faced him. "You have to guess."

"To see Santa Claus."

"Nooo," she said. "How could we go see Santa Clause? He comes in the winter. It's not winter. It's summer. We went to see my Grandma and we picked strawberries."

"Did you pick a lot?"

"Yes I did. I picked a real lot. I picked the most for a little girl. My mama's proud of me."

Johnny smiled slightly. "Is she?"

"Yes, she's proud of me. I'm proud of her too."

As he often did after seeing Marlianna, Johnny thought involuntarily of her father. Raymond Keller had been in a serious accident four years ago, just after Marlianna's birth. He was now in a wheelchair and had memory problems. Johnny wished he could learn to talk to Marlianna without always being reminded of the accident. When she left, walking away singing "we want Marky Bear, we want Marky Bear" over and over, Johnny went into the house to find lunch. He looked at the leftover pea soup in the refrigerator, then fixed himself a bowl of ice cream and a plate of cookies. *Wheat and milk*, he thought. *That's healthy*. As he ate he watched a TV show on exploring the Arctic, noticing how much blue there was in the scenes.

At the end of August, on an unusually clear, sunny day, neither hot nor humid, Johnny drove through the hills of central Pennsylvania, through the village of Huntingdon, then out to Big Valley, where Leah and Addie lived. Johnny was always glad to see his sister, who he loved and always talked to more openly and deeply than he talked to anyone else. Back when he was twenty-two and had fallen in love with Melanie, he would write her letters, and when she didn't reply right away, he would hurry to his sister to ask why the woman he was in love with hadn't answered yet. Eventually he and Melanie would marry, but early in the relationship, when he wondered what was happening, when he was frantic that Melanie didn't call, when he was grieved that she said she was busy and couldn't go to a movie, when he wondered how serious she was about him, Johnny had gone to Leah.

As he drove out to Big Valley, Johnny had to slow down three times to go around the horse-drawn carriages of Amish families. In the long driveway up to Leah's house, her husband, Jake, was standing by the fruit trees that lined the drive, picking apples and putting them in a basket.

"Good crop there?" Johnny called to his brother-in-law.

"Good enough for pies," Jake said, holding up an apple. "I'll be up to the house after I pick some of these that've fallen down."

Leah sat on the back porch with a glass of German white wine, the only kind she would drink. Johnny came through the house and found her there. "You need fortification?" she asked, slightly lifting her glass.

Before Johnny answered they watched Addie kick a large rubber ball in the backyard.

"Look how fast I kick it!" she cried. "Look how fast!" She kicked the ball off into a row of forsythia, now full covered with green leaves. "Ha ha ha!" Addie laughed and chased after the ball. When she reached the ball she turned toward the house and yelled, "Mama! I kicked it really fast!"

"You sure did," Leah called back.

"Yeah, I did!" To most people outside the family, the sight of a nineteen-year-old girl acting like Addie would have seemed awkward and sad, but Leah and Johnny had watched Addie's body grow into adulthood while her mind avoided that trauma, and they were accustomed to her. Johnny had sometimes marveled at the grace his sister had shown in the love she gave to her daughter.

After a glass of wine with Leah, Johnny said, "I finished the picture. You want to see it?"

"What picture?" she asked, but the way she tilted her head forward and looked expectant when she said this made Johnny think she knew which one.

"Your portrait," he said. "I finished it a few days ago. I was waiting for it to dry to bring it out. You want to see it?"

"Sure. I posed for it."

He went back to the car to get the painting. The wall behind Leah in the portrait was a deep yellow, almost gold, with hints of orange. Most of Johnny's portraits placed the subject in a generally empty background, so that the eye of the viewer focused completely on the person in the picture. In this case, however, he had decided to include a small basket with apples. He wanted the picture to capture something of Leah's life. In many of his memories his sister was cutting up green apples, making blueberry jam, butchering a bloody rabbit.

Johnny looked at Leah studying the picture, then glanced down at it. In the picture, light coming in the window was backlighting the figure, so that the light played around her hair.

Finally Leah looked up. "It makes me look too good," she said.

"This is how you look," he replied.

"Yes," she said slowly, then was silent a few seconds. "Of course it's me, but there's something about it. I don't know what it is, but it makes me seem better than I am. I don't mean more attractive. You definitely caught every wrinkle under my eyes."

"Maybe you don't like it that it shows you just sitting," Johnny said. "You're always so busy."

"No, no. It's...it's like you don't know any bad things about me."

"I grew up with you. I guess I know some bad things."

"You probably don't know the worst."

"Well, I—"

She laid the picture on the table and turned around to look at him. "There's things nobody knows. I've been thinking a lot about this lately." She stopped and smiled with one side of her mouth, a sad smile, as if she were smiling at irony. "Maybe it's because soon I won't be able to tell anybody what I've done. I need to tell somebody."

Johnny hated conversations when they referred to Leah dying. He knew it was childish of him, but he could hardly bear these talks. For all the strength and decisiveness that Leah had always provided, it was frightening to talk of her death.

She stared at him with her serious gray-green eyes. "Do this for me, Johnny," she said. "Let me tell you."

He tightened his lips and sat down. "Tell me anything you want," he said. With his hands together in his lap, he stared at her.

"Alright. When I was thirteen, I stole Mama's earrings, the ones with little emeralds. Do you remember them?"

"No." This wasn't as serious as he had expected. "But why did you steal them?"

"I just wanted to wear them to school one day, to show off in front of the other girls. I didn't really mean to steal them, just borrow them, but can you believe how stupid I was? I lost them before I even got to school. I never told Mama, never told anybody."

"Kids do stupid things," Johnny said.

"Mama was so upset, and I felt really guilty that I didn't tell her."

Johnny pursed his lips and frowned slightly. "That was a long time ago. Is it really bothering you that much?"

"No, not so much anymore."

Johnny nodded and smiled at his sister.

She hesitated, then glanced toward the door. As she spoke, she leaned forward slightly and lowered her voice. "This is just information for you, you know," she said.

Johnny looked at her, his smile slowly fading as he studied her expression and then nodded.

"I need to tell this," Leah said. She glanced at the door again. "About ten years ago, when I was feeling really frustrated with Addie, and feeling like life at home had just gone to hell, taking some frustration out on Jake, I met somebody." She stopped, but Johnny didn't say anything. "I met somebody, and for a while I forgot about how tough it was at home. I had an affair for three months."

Johnny hoped he didn't look surprised, but he felt it. Leah and Jake had always seemed good together. For a second, he wondered if she was joking, but she obviously wasn't. "This happens to people," he said. "I guess you're not the first."

"And probably not the last," she replied.

No, not the first or the last. People have brief affairs all the time, but as Johnny drove home, he was irritated with himself for feeling disturbed. What Leah had done was wrong, but it was over long ago, and he knew that things had been good with Jake after that.

For the next two months Johnny was trying to finish a series of nature paintings for a show at a museum in Cleveland. On a warmish afternoon in late October, with his window open, he was in the room where he painted, studying the picture he was working on. He looked at a spot where a grayish green and rusty red came together. He wasn't sure he liked the contrast and squinted at it.

"Hey! Hey!" He heard his little neighbor Marlianna calling. "Where are you?"

He broke away from the painting and went to the window. "Marlianna," he called.

"Where are you?" she asked again.

"I'm inside working."

"You want to come out? I can't see you."

"I'm at the window here." A moment later Marlianna came around the building, shuffling through the dead leaves lying in the yard. With her was her dog, a small beagle, an old dog that walked slowly at her side.

"Oh, *now* I see you," she said. "You want to come out? I saw a rabbit. Barty wouldn't chase it. I could show it to you."

"I'd like to see the rabbit," Johnny said, "but I've got to work."

"Oh." Marlianna pulled a tall weed that had grown up in the flowerbed. "What are you working?" She flapped the weed back and forth.

"I'm painting," Johnny told her. "I'm painting pictures of flowers."

"Can I see?"

"They're not done yet. I'm not ready to show them to anybody."

Marlianna threw the weed down and said, "I like real flowers."

"There's still some flowers in my flowerbed," Johnny said. "You can have some flowers."

"Can I pick some flowers?"

"Yeah, pick your mother a nice bouquet. You know where they are?"

"Over there?" She pointed across the yard.

"Yep. You can pick yourself some flowers, and I've got to go back to painting, so I'll talk to you later."

"OK."

Johnny returned to his painting, looked at it, and decided to paint over the green with a dark brown. Later, when he left the house to go to the store, he found a bundle of chrysanthemums tied together with a piece of grass, lying on the small table on the porch next to the front door.

The November hills of central Pennsylvania had moved into shades of brown. Johnny stood by a window at Leah and

Jake's house, in a room with a wall of windows overlooking their vegetable garden. The plot was filled now with overgrown tomato and zucchini plants, turning brown and interspersed with weeds. Beyond the garden was a field that had stood green with soybeans all summer, and farther on, a ridge of hills ran along the edge of Big Valley.

Johnny turned toward Leah, who was sitting in a chair by the window. She had her eyes closed and her back to the window. Addie, who had been playing in the den next door, entered the room.

"I can't find cartoons," she said.

Leah opened her eyes. "Honey, they're on channel thirty-four."

"I looked on channel thirteen four." Addie had her lower lip out. "I looked. I looked there."

"Well, they're…" Leah looked at her brother, then said to Addie, "Come here sweetie."

Addie walked over and knelt down by her mother. Leah put her arms around her and kissed her on the cheek. "Uncle Johnny is going to help you find cartoons. Aren't you, Uncle Johnny?"

"Sure," Johnny said. "I love cartoons."

"Me too," Addie declared. "We like cartoons, don't we, Uncle Johnny."

"Yes, we do. Let's see what we can find."

Johnny changed the TV to the correct channel and Addie sat happily on the couch with a glass of juice. For a few minutes he sat with her, she snuggled up against him, and together they watched SpongeBob SquarePants. After the first cartoon, Addie said, "He's not real, is he?"

"He's a real cartoon," Johnny replied. He looked out the window and saw his brother-in-law riding on the blue tractor, turning past some trees and headed toward the barn. It was a cold day and unpleasant to be out in the chill wind, but it was also bright sunny weather. More trees would stand stark by evening,

288

as the wind was thrashing branches, attempting to strip off the remaining leaves.

Two weeks later all the trees stretched bare to the cold sky, and the land seemed closed and immobile. A month further on, a wet January snow fell, drifting down softly until it lined every branch. The sight was so sublime it almost justified all the bitter chill of winter.

Johnny had walked out into the yard to immerse himself in the stunning vision of this snowfall. He breathed in the cold air, pulled his hat down lower on his ears, and walked farther down his driveway, looking at the trees as he went. Suddenly he bent down and scooped up snow, formed it into a ball, and tossed it toward a tree. The snowball went past the tree and disappeared into the whiteness beyond it. Again he made a snowball and aimed at the tree, this time smacking it against the trunk.

"You got it!" a high voice cried out happily. Johnny turned and saw Marlianna, bundled up in a bright white outfit, almost invisible against the snow. "You hit the tree!"

"Hello, Marlianna!" Johnny called. "You like this snow?"

"Yeah."

Johnny smiled and asked, "You want to have a snowball fight?"

"Noooo! You'll win!"

"OK," he said. He saw the tracks of her dog, and asked, "Is Barty with you?"

"He's inside," she replied. "He doesn't like the cold."

Johnny nodded. "Let's make snow angels," he suggested.

Marlianna frowned exaggeratedly. "Snow *angels*? How can you make a angel out of snow?"

"You never made a snow angel?"

"I don't think I did it. I never thought I made one."

"Oh, then I have to show you how to make a snow angel. All little girls are supposed to know how to make snow angels."

"OK, I want to make one. Is it like a real angel?"

"No, these just look like angels. You have to use your imagination." Johnny walked into the yard, to a wide spot by the forsythia bushes. He turned to Marlianna. "Alright. Watch me do it. You have to fall back in the snow." He spread both arms out straight to his side, then fell backwards. "Now," he said, lying in the snow, "you move your legs back and forth…" and he moved his legs out to the side then back together in the middle, "and you move your arms up and down…" and he slid both outstretched arms up and down along the ground beside him, "so when you get up, you have an angel." He stood carefully, and where he had been lying was the shape he had left on the ground.

"Hey!" Marlianna cried. "You did make a angel! I want to do it."

"OK, hold your arms out, and fall backwards. Don't worry, the snow is soft."

She fell back like an expert, then imitated what she had seen him do. When she stood, they looked down to where an adult angel and a child angel had been lying on the ground. He studied Marlianna, standing snow-covered, sunlight gleaming off her white winter outfit. She was looking up at him with snow in her hair and a huge smile.

The snow of the snow angels was followed three days later by sleet. The winter was snowier than usual, and maybe colder too. Johnny wasn't comparing temperatures to years past, but he thought he felt colder, even though he was wearing three layers of clothing. And was his house always so chilly? He bought a small electric heater to use in the room where he painted, placing it next to the old yellow couch where he took naps in the afternoon.

By the middle of cold white February, Leah had grown so ill that she now spent most of her time either in bed or lying back in a chair. Because it was winter, Jake had little to do outside on the farm, so he could care for both Leah and Addie. Several times a week when Johnny drove over, Leah was sitting in the den looking out the windows, wrapped in a maroon covering their aunt had crocheted years before. It wasn't that she was cold all the time, but she began treating the old maroon cover the way a child treats a favorite blanket. On a Thursday Johnny drove past the house and through Belleville, on out to Peachy's store, to buy a cake for her. He chose a pumpkin rollup with a cream filling, knowing this was something she especially liked.

As he drove up to Jake and Leah's house, Johnny thought about Leah's revelation about having an affair. Did that mean she had stopped loving Jake? Johnny paused before getting out of the car, with this thought in his mind. No, he decided, it didn't mean that. Whatever it meant, she still loved Jake. Leah had even told Johnny in the years after her affair that marriage is worth it, in spite of the bad things. She told him this when his own marriage to Melanie was ending, when Melanie decided to leave him.

Coming into the house, he found his sister in the den, looking out the window, a frequent activity for her now. "Leah

293

Rae," he said, using her full name, something he had done occasionally since they were children.

She turned around, and he saw that her tired eyes looked red, but she smiled when she saw him.

"It's really cold out," Johnny said. "They're predicting more snow tonight. I've got an igloo started in the back yard, in case I need to move out there."

"You're not the igloo type," she said, and laughed. "You need comfort."

"I can tolerate adversity if I have to."

"Maybe," she replied, looking at him doubtfully. "But you don't have to."

"You criticize my survival skills, yet I've brought you an excess of sugar." He held up the cake.

"And baked in your own igloo. Cut me a piece."

Johnny took the cake to the kitchen, where Jake was peeling potatoes. "Don't let Addie see that," he told Johnny, "or I'll never get her to eat any dinner."

294

"I'll stick the rest in the cabinet." Johnny said. Taking a plate with a piece of the cake, he went back out to the den.

Leah thanked him and took a few greedy bites, savoring the flavor and richness of the cake and filling. "You're being very nice," she told her brother.

"Haven't I always been like that?" he asked.

"I just wanted to tell you I'm noticing." She took another bite of cake, then looked out the window for a minute. Still looking out the window, she asked, "Do you remember when I told you about taking Mama's earrings?"

"Yes, you're still guilty about losing them."

"Not just that, but I never told her. And…" she paused. "Would you shut the door?"

With a sudden feeling of unpleasant anticipation, he got up and closed it.

"And what I said about being with someone?"

"Yes."

Again there was a silence while she looked out the window. "There's more I want to tell you."

"Tell me anything you want," he said, wishing badly that she wouldn't.

"I appreciate you listening," she told him, and smiled slightly, but the faint smile was quickly gone. "Several years ago I shot a neighbor's cat. It was stalking birds at our bird feeder, and I tried for three weeks to scare it off. I mean, I did a lot of things to get rid of it, but nothing worked, and then I found a dead golden-winged warbler, one of my favorite songbirds, lying by the back steps. And the next time I saw that cat crouched under the feeder, I got the 22."

"I think you had cause to shoot it," Johnny said. "Some people would think this is pretty bad, I guess, but I don't."

"I thought you'd feel that way. I'm just trying to get my courage up. But I've got to tell you something that there's no excusing. There's just no way around it." She looked heavily serious now. "Jake knows about it, by the way, but nobody else."

She looked grim as she spoke.

"I don't want to ask you to forgive this, or try to understand it, nothing like that. And maybe I shouldn't put this on you, and I won't if you don't want me to."

"No, I'll listen."

She sighed. "Really, Johnny, it's bad, and if you don't want to hear it."

"Tell me," he said.

She waited, then said, "It was about four years ago. I was coming home from Deena's birthday party, maybe ten o'clock at night. I hadn't really wanted to stay that late, but because Deena had helped me with Addie that week, I thought I should help her clean up. Because I stayed to help her, we were talking and while we talked she opened another bottle of wine, so I'm sure I had more to drink than I should have. I didn't feel drunk really, you know how it is when you've had several drinks in a nice setting, you just feel relaxed and happy. I was glad to be feeling that way, not worrying so much about things, the way I usually do. But still..." She stopped, looking sad, and shook her head. "I just thought I'd be a little more careful, and it was only five miles on country roads."

Johnny was staring at her, compelled by the story to listen, but not wanting to hear it.

Leah glanced at him, then looked away as she spoke. "With a beginning like this, you can probably pretty easy figure more or less where it goes. I wasn't in an accident, of course. You'd remember if I had been. When I was coming down School House Road toward 655, and it seemed fine... I don't know." She stopped. "It was... I guess, I don't know, maybe I was looking at the radio." She paused again. "I just... suddenly there were headlights right in front of me, coming right at me. I swerved over, to the right, and I thought I'd go in the ditch, but when I swerved over, I was in my lane." She sighed. "The other car swerved too, and went off the road. At first, I thought they must be OK. I had swerved over, and I was OK, so I thought that we'd both just had a close call. Then I saw from the lights in my rearview mirror that the car was off the road. But I was driving along, and... I did a terrible thing, Johnny. I just kept driving. I started shaking so much I had to slow down and could hardly drive, but I kept going. I felt so weak and shaky I wasn't sure I could even drive. The next day I heard that Raymond Keller was injured, and from the location I knew he was driving the car that I ran off the road."

Raymond Keller. Marlianna's father. No one ever knew who had run him off the road, who had caused the wreck that had left him suffering from memory problems and in a wheelchair. Leah had put him there. She turned away from the window now and faced him. Tears were running down her face. "I never told anybody," she said, and began sobbing, softly at first, then harder.

Johnny leaned forward and put his arms around her.

For Leah's funeral a month later, the weather was unusually warm. Johnny and Jake were able to stand at the grave wearing nothing heavier than their dark suit coats. Addie had remained at the house with a neighbor, as they thought she wouldn't understand and would become overly upset. Afterward, when most of the mourners had left the grave, Jake and Johnny still stood there. Jake looked hollow-eyed and banished into permanent sadness. Johnny saw this and felt heavy with sympathy for his brother-in-law, but his own feeling of loss was so intense that it was hard to forget about himself.

All of his life he had talked to Leah about what he should do. What should he do now?

Other than the fate of Addie, nothing interested Johnny. He didn't care that the sun remained warm, or that over the next several days a few buds began to come out. He didn't care that a new book on contemporary artists had called him a unique visual voice creating his own language. He didn't care whether he ate or that the pot of beef stew had been in the refrigerator for five days.

Several days after the funeral, he was coming home from the drugstore when he saw Marlianna sitting on a bench near the edge of her yard. She appeared to be crying. For the first time in several days Johnny was able to turn his attention away from his own feelings, and he stopped the car and got out.

"Marlianna," he said, "are you OK? Did you get hurt?"

"N- n- no," she replied, catching heavy breaths.

"You're not OK?" he asked again. "Are you hurt?"

"No," she cried. "Our dog died. He was old and he died. But I liked him. Daddy said I can get another dog, but I liked Barty."

"I'm sorry, honey," Johnny said, kneeling down. "I'm sorry Barty died. It's sad when you love your dog and he dies. But when you get another dog, I'll help you teach him tricks. I know some tricks for dogs."

She looked at him and stopped crying for a moment. "OK," she said, but tears were rolling down her cheeks.

That afternoon, Johnny walked in his yard, thinking about the conversation with Marlianna. She was so upset over the death of her pet, pouring out her emotions more openly and naturally than Johnny had done over Leah. Maybe that was a difference between adults and children. Maybe it was how he had grown up. Or maybe it was just him. It wasn't that he didn't feel a deep emptiness. Leah was such a sweet, kind person, as good a person as he'd ever known. But as he thought this, he remembered her sitting in a chair in her den, covered with a crocheted maroon blanket, telling him about running Marlianna's father off the road, putting him in a wheelchair, never telling anyone.

Johnny put up his hand to block the sunlight from his eyes. It was warm and bright today. He looked at the bushes in front of him, the forsythia bushes, and saw that tiny buds had begun to form on the branches. Next to these bushes was where he and Marlianna had made the snow angels. He stood next to the bushes, looking at the ground, his mind swirling, trying to think of something that made sense.

CPSIA information can be obtained at www.ICGtesting.com
Printed in the USA
LVOW10s0844011016

506776LV00010B/5/P